Turning the Page

Olivia Gaines

I can't help it; I love with my everything.

Olivia Gaines

Olivia Gaines

Davonshire House Publishing
PO Box 9716
Augusta, GA 30916

This book is a work of fiction. Names, characters, places and incidents are products of the author's vivid imagination or are used fictitiously. Any resemblance to actual events, locales or persons, living or dead, is entirely a coincidence.

The Fool Speaks of Love, based on *The Negro Speaks of Rivers*, is printed and featured with the approval of Mark Peacock,

© 2015 Olivia Gaines, Cheryl Aaron Corbin

Copy Editor: Teresa Blackwell
Cover: koou-graphics
Olivia Gaines Make Up and Photograph by Latasla Gardner Photography

ASIN:

ISBN-13: 978-0692502327

ISBN-10:0692502327
All rights reserved. No part of this book may be reproduced in any form or by any means whatsoever. For information address, Davonshire House Publishing, PO Box 9716, Augusta, GA 30916.

Printed in the United States of America
1 2 3 4 5 6 7 10 9 8

First Davonshire House Publishing June2015

DEDICATION

For Mark who reminded me of the importance of bringing the words to life with one single wildflower which will forever be pressed between my pages.

Olivia Gaines

ACKNOWLEDGMENTS

To all the fans, friends and supporters of the dream as well as the Facebook community of writers who keep me focused, inspired and moving forward.

Write On!

Augusta Writers
Est 2009

Olivia Gaines

"Easy reading is damn hard writing."

- Nathaniel Hawthorne

Also by Olivia Gaines

The Slice of Life Series

- The Perfect Man
- Friends with Benefits
- A Letter to My Mother
- The Basement of Mr. McGee
- A New Mommy for Christmas

The Slivers of Love Series

- The Cost to Play
- Thursday in Savannah
- Girl's Weekend
- Beneath the Well of Dawn
- Santa's Big Helper

The Davonshire Series

- Courting Guinevere
- Loving Words
- Vanity's Pleasure

The Blakemore Files

- Being Mrs. Blakemore
- Shopping with Mrs. Blakemore
- Dancing with Mr. Blakemore
- Cruising with the Blakemores
- Dinner with the Blakemores

The Value of a Man Series

- My Mail Order Wife

Other Novellas

- North to Alaska
- The Brute & The Blogger
- A Better Night in Vegas (Betas Do It Better Anthology)

Turning the Page

I recently had the pleasure of being a student again in a Harlem Renaissance Class where we focused a great deal on the works of Langston Hughes. One of our writing assignments was to create our own version of *The Negro Speaks of Rivers*. My fellow classmates did a fantastic job with this project, but one of the works spoke to me. Please allow me the honor of introducing you to this very talented young man. Ladies and gentlemen, Mr. Mark Peacock.

The Fool Speaks of Love

By Mark Peacock

I've known love:
I've known love ancient as the vastness of the universe and older than the
    flow of rivers in the Garden of Eden.

My soul has been intoxicated by the potency of love.

I bathed in the poison that had touched Romeo's lips.
I built my army in the attempt to bring my dear Helen back from Troy and it drove me mad.
I looked upon the Yamuna River and raised the Taj Mahal above it.
I heard the singing of the Sirens when Odysseus
    was tied to the mast of his ship, and I've seen their luring
    enchant turn the waters crimson in the fading of the sun.

I've known love:
Breathing, pulsating love.

My soul has been intoxicated by the potency of love.

MAPeacock@gru.edu

Olivia Gaines

Turning the Page

This is Janie and Ethan, two bookstore owners. Go ahead, turn the page so that we may begin their story.

Olivia Gaines

Chapter 1. But Janie... I love you.

    Jimmy Earl found a reason six days of the week to come into Janie's bookstore. Most days, it was simply to sit and stare at the object of his affection. Other days, it was to ask out the entity of his desire, only to be gently let down then sent on his way. It did little good because every day, the silly man came back, his heart upon his sleeve and sad puppy dog eyes that lapped her up like a cool drink of water on a hot autumn evening. He was just one more nuisance on the bookshelf of her life. Jimmy Earl sat as a constant reminder of something else that often needed to be pulled down and dusted off because it was stuck on the back rack of her mind; her love life.

    Love was something Janie Cimoc had neither the time nor any use for; well, not in this life anyway. In this life, the small bookstore she owned supported her family. A rather large family headed by parents who spent too much time cultivating a lucrative plant they rarely sold but found it necessary to sample – daily. Her three brothers helped in and around the shop while her sister worked shifts on the cash register. The one good thing about working with her family, if anyone stole out the register, no one would eat. Every penny earned in the little bookshop either went to put a roof over their heads, food in their bellies, or clothes and shoes on the bodies that lived in the tin-roofed trailer the Cimoc's called home. Janie didn't live with her family; she lived in her bookstore.

    The Comic Book was her life. It was also the only place where the insanity of the Cimoc family did not threaten to overrun the small peace of mind she garnered from ownership of the shabby little shop that was given to her by the former owner, Cecil Habersham. Cecil was a gentle giant that spent more time preparing for ComicCon than he did running the business. At 16, Janie started working in the shop to make some money to pay for the things she needed for school. Soon, she found she was buying a couple of chickens and a sack of potatoes to make sure there was some dinner in the Cimoc house. It bothered her far more than she cared to admit that at the age of 17, she knew more about foreclosure procedures than she should. Her quickly gained knowledge saved them from being tossed on the streets multiple times due to some unforeseen deficiency of monies her parents couldn't seem to understand.

Her parents, Edward and Alice Cimoc, were, well...hippies. The small plot of land on which the trailer they owned stood, grew many of the vegetables the family ate. The few egg laying chickens they possessed provided fresh eggs, but in a very hard year, a cold snap came through suddenly, and all the birds were frozen to death. This also lay the ground work for the shortage of funds that never seemed to re-accumulate. Each day was a struggle. Even more so for Janie.

As the eldest of five, she often would forgo meals to make sure her brothers and sisters had enough to eat so their little brains could fully develop. Most days, Mr. Habersham understood her hunger and would bring an extra plate of food to the store. She ate well at least three days out of the week. The older she became, the more Mr. Habersham traveled. Six years ago, after leaving HeroesCon, he fell in love with a woman who role played as the Warrior Princess, complete with full costume. Cecil returned to his little shop, called his attorney, and signed everything over to Janie.

Janie stood on the stoop of The Comic Book watching Cecil drive away with all of his costumes, gaming gear, and notepads boxed away in the back of his Dodge Ram on his way to Denver. As much as he had taught her in five years about the business, he still had not taught her bookkeeping. That part of the daily operations was a sore spot. It was still unclear how to balance the books, but somehow, Janie had managed to keep her head above water for six years.

Her first year, she succeeded in obtaining a local graphic designer to teach a workshop at the store. It was such a success that the used book section that occupied way too much floor space was dismantled to make room for other special projects and classes in the shop. The bookshelves were moved and left a great deal of open space that now was well lit to reveal many years of dirt and grime and that weird smell which would not go away. Ironically, she always thought the smell was Mr. Habersham, but he had been gone six months, and the funk didn't seem to dissipate. Janie and her brother Holden employed some elbow grease to clear away the dirty old tiles from the filth-ridden floor and added some air fresheners and plants to help filter the air. The sale of the old books brought in enough cash to buy some discounted tiles from the local home repair store. Holden, who was younger than Janie by two years, was a pretty handy type of guy and very good with his hands. He was also a very visual learner, so with the aid of a couple of online videos, he managed to lay the tile better than a professional. Holden also had a keen sense of observation and a bit of an affliction with OCD, which greatly helped. Janie loved how beautiful ideas could form when given the right motivation, and Holden was inspired to do more. Enlisting the help of their younger brother Jem, he set to work on repairing the rundown house the family called home.

As her sister Meg got older, she too wanted to earn a few dollars and learn how to be more self-sufficient. Janie handed Meg a book on accounting and investing, and within a year, the business was in the black. A few more tables were added to the rear of the store for when the local Dungeons and Dragons groups met. The idea went over well. Johnny, the youngest brother, was big into anime. He suggested that on Saturday afternoons he and his friends could use the back tables to play Yu-gi-O. Janie had no idea what that was, but Meg suggested charging the kids $5 a piece to enter the gaming area to make a few extra bucks. Holden built in shelves to hold board games for Thursday night gaming. Johnny suggested Holden also build a tabletop for miniatures for gamers on Friday nights. Before her eyes, and with the assistance of some very detailed videos, Holden recreated Middle Earth on a six foot banquet table.

Every Wednesday through Saturday evening, parents knew where to find their geeky young children. It was a safe environment for the kids to hang out, and the few bucks Janie charged was paid with pleasure by parents who often donated cookies or snacks for Friday and Saturday game play. The Mayor even came in one Saturday and donated $100 for prizes for tournament winners.

Yes, Janie's comic book store was loved by the community. So was Janie. She was especially loved by Jimmy Earl. He was still in the shop, sitting at the table, one hand above it, the other under it. She paid him no mind, but Holden did.

He yelled at the odd little man, "Jimmy Earl, get your crap and get outta here right now. Go on! Git!"

As he scuttled past Janie, Jimmy Earl tried to rub against her backside, but Holden was faster. "If I see you anywhere near my sister, I am going to put my fist in your face!"

Jimmy Earl was highly upset. "Janie! How can you allow him to speak to me this way? Especially after everything we are to each other!"

The responsive expression which covered her face answered Holden's question. This man was nothing more than a perverted nuisance. "Jimmy Earl, don't make me call the Sheriff!"

"You can call anybody you like, Holden Cimoc, but that is not going to change my feelings. Janie," he said. "I love you. I ain't afraid to confess my yearning for you. Your golden hair. Those sweet lips...your perky bosom...you are my..."

He never got to finish the sentence. Holden pushed him out of the shop and locked the door. "Janie, if that creep comes back in here, I am going to beat his ass, then call the cops. Stop allowing him through the door. He may get up his courage when none of us are around and try something."

Janie only smiled as she patted her brother on the back. "Well, if that is the case, I am safe. You guys are always around."

That was also part of the problem. She had no romantic life because her family was always in the middle of everything. Each time a guy tried to spend some time and get close, either a brother or a sister would poke their heads into the conversation. "Things will only change when you make a change, Janie girl," her mom would always tell her.

Right now, she was going to change a pillowcase and stick her face in it. "Thanks, Holden," she told her brother as she locked the door behind him. She switched off the lights and made a slow climb up the stairs to the apartment over the shop. It wasn't much, but with some handiwork from Jem and Holden, it was far better than she could have hoped.

Dinner tonight was leftover spaghetti that Meg had brought her from home, along with a side salad. It was food, nothing fancy, but to her it was a feast.

"For this meal, I give thanks," she said. It was a ritual she never allowed to pass. In her mind, nothing scars a child worse than hunger. Janie had spent many a night going to bed hungry. Each meal she ate was a blessing. More blessings were about to come her way as well, in means and manners it would take her a lifetime to comprehend.

Chapter 2. Welcome to Bartleby's…

Ethan Strom entered the bookstore through the back door; the same way he did each morning. The leather crossbody bag slung across his mid-section was the first thing he dropped on the counter as he washed his hands and prepared the first pot of coffee. It was the last Monday of the month. Tonight was the meeting of the romance book club.

Tomorrow, it was the young adult book club meeting. This was followed on Wednesday with the non-fiction book club, the Thursday thriller readers, and the Friday mainstream fiction clubs. The monthly book clubs at Bartleby's were a joy to host as well as a serious revenue generator. Ethan knew how many members were in each book club, which made ordering inventory a breeze. He only needed to stay two months ahead of the readers, which kept him three months ahead of the bankers. His bookstore was a gem in the mid-sized college town of Venture, Georgia.

Henry Strom, his father, moved to Venture when he and his sister were only kids. His sister Tallulah was only older by three years and now one of the town's two pediatricians. Like most things in Venture, there were two of everything, one white and the other not white. It didn't bother Ethan much; he really loved Venture. So did Henry.

The initial job offered to the Reverend Doctor Strom was to take over a small ministry at the Greater Mount Zion Baptist Church. Initially, Henry was told the congregation was topping out at nearly 100 parishioners. Well, that was the number on the roster for the church members; the number of bodies in the pews was actually ten. Three of them, Pastor Strom was certain, showed up to have a new place to nap. It wouldn't have been so insulting if those three members of the congregation didn't snore. Yet, the reverend took it in stride.

"Son, with perseverance, determination, and a plan, a vision can come to life," he told Ethan.

Ethan used these same words to open Bartleby's after he graduated college. At 24 years old, he was a small business owner. If fate had been kind, he would have preferred to attend graduate school and become a librarian; instead, he fell in love with his bookstore and began developing his vision. The shelves were stocked with the works of famous writers, but he had a story in his head that would not go away. During quiet moments in the bookstore, he took time to ponder over words that eventually formed into a paragraph. The paragraphs became chapters, and slowly a rough draft of a novel was born. The only problem with the story was that Ethan hated it.

The novel was pretty much symbolic of his life and the bookstore: shiny and everything perfectly aligned for the public. The reality, which slapped him across the head twice a day, was the sameness that threatened to consume his sanity. The novel was flat and lacking any standout characterization. Also, like his life. The truth, like a classic novel, was filled with foils, too much structure, and choked by the mundane. Ethan Strom knew his life was strangling him with mundanity.

His vision for the bookstore was to have something out of the norm. For the most part, he had succeeded. His store was the only shop in town that served Artesian coffees rarely found in a town this far south or of this size.

Gourmet coffees like Palheta's Bouquet or Sumatran Gayo were rotated in the shop and the locals loved it. They also loved Ethan. He had a quiet confidence that was never imposing or impeding. He treated everyone the same, whether he liked them or not.

"Earth to Ethan," Tallulah said to him over dinner on Sunday night. "Is everything okay? You seem to be off in your head somewhere."

"I'm fine. Just planning out some ideas," he told both her and his parents.

Ironically, he gave the same answer the following Saturday night to his...he wasn't sure what Kate was to him. They went out on a date a year ago and she kept coming back whether he invited her or not. Kate, in his mind, was a supporting character with no real purpose other than to push along his storyline. He wasn't even certain if he liked the woman, but she represented an ideal to him that also roiled about in his head.

Kate was a librarian. She was also a quite an accomplished poet. She boasted often about being published in several poetry magazines. In her head, it was a foregone conclusion they were going to be married; she was waiting for him to propose and present her with a ring. Kate would be waiting a very long time since Ethan had no intention of a long term relationship with her. He would rather sit and watch the pile of dog poo from his neighbor's mutt solidify and turn white.

Kate was an attractive black woman with generous hips and full lips that were always correcting him about something he was doing that was not to her satisfaction.

"Honestly, Ethan, sometimes I don't know why I put up with you," Kate told him.

Turning the Page

Ethan parked his Ford in front of her pretty yellow cottage that was surrounded by more flowers than a cemetery. His clear eyes gazed upon her in the dimly lit car, asking her, "Really?"

"Yes, really. I mean it has been a year...I don't know where this or we are going for that matter..." Kate said emphatically.

It was time to turn the page on this chapter of their story. It was dull and uninspired and he wanted to trade it in for something more interesting. "You are right, Kate. I have been selfish," he told her.

Kate leaned back in the seat, pleased as grape punch with lemons floating on top. The expression on her face implied she had struck a nerve and the relationship was about to make a drastic move. She was right.

"I'm sorry, Kate. I have been selfishly occupying your time and Saturday nights with my needs and have been ignorant of your own. I know you want to be married and have children," he said softly.

Kate's eyes were tearful as she faced him in the late model Ford. "For that reason Kate, I am going to step out of your life," Ethan said.

Her eyebrows went up as if she misunderstood what he said. To ensure she was understanding the simple plot twist, he spoke slowly, "I am not ready to get married nor have kids. It is not fair of me to bogard your affections knowing we don't want the same things. I am sorry. I will no longer be selfish. I am going to reluctantly let us end," he said.

The left side of his face stung all the way home from the hard slap she gave him. Kate hit him with such force that his mouth started to salivate, leaving him able to taste what he had for lunch seven hours ago. That pain would go away. Spending another minute in her company was an eternal pain that sapped him of energy each time he was in her company. Letting her go was most unselfish thing he had ever done in his life.

Ethan Strom, at heart, was a hopeless romantic. He wanted the type of love that he'd read about in the classics. His heart craved the kind of love that a man would forfeit his crown to possess. He desired a woman who gave him goose pimples whenever his fingers made contact with her skin, asking him to belong to her alone.

He wanted a love that would make him grow. In the interim, he had to find a way to make his business grow so he would have a future to offer a woman. In his gut was the niggling feeling that the woman he needed was about to create a new scenario in his story, and he could not wait to read what happened next.

Chapter 3. A New Chapter...

At first, Ethan thought it was someone playing a joke on him. He almost hung up the phone when the nasally caricatured voice came across the line telling him, "Please hold the line for a call from Mayor Galley."

Why would the Mayor be calling me? The Mayor's booming baritone came across the line with his deep Southern drawl.

"Ethan, my boy, something of grave importunacy has come across my desk. I do not like it, nor do I desire for it to come to fruition," Mayor Galley told him.

The one-sided conversation continued for several more minutes before Mayor Galley asked, "Do you understand what I am saying, Son?"

No, I don't.

"Good. I will see you in my office at 11 am sharp! I have meetings all day so do not be late," he told him.

Ethan hung up the phone. As he stood behind the counter, a perplexed look covered his face. His mother, a quiet woman born to be church first lady, watched him closely.

"Is there something wrong, Ethan?" Hester Strom wanted to know.

"I was summoned to the Mayor's office today for a meeting at 11," he told his mother.

Hester checked her watch. "You only have a half hour. Since you don't have time to call anyone in to cover the shop, I will stay and handle things for you," Hester said.

"Thanks, Mom, that means a lot," he told her. The great thing was, his Mom came to the bookstore every Wednesday for a cup of Palheta's Bouquet. One day, Ethan was slow getting the dark brew started, and his mother learned how to operate the coffee machine. Since she was in the shop each Wednesday anyway, Ethan trained her to man the register, stock shelves, receive inventory, and update the POS system. Leaving his mother in charge of the shop was an easy thing to do. Getting through the next few hours he found to be more than taxing on his patience, his nerves, and his eyeballs.

Janie didn't really know what to make of Mayor Galley's request to come to his office. She was told to be there at 11 am sharp. Dressed and ready to head out the door, she stopped briefly to update her brother. Jem was out of school and able to man the store for her in the morning, and Meg would be in at noon to start her shift.

Not quite certain what to wear, as well as having no fashion sense whatsoever, Janie donned her favorite pink tee shirt and a loose fitting pair of gym pants and headed to her meeting. Once she arrived, she immediately understood her favorite tee was probably not the best choice of clothing. This became evident when a black man standing in front of the Mayor's office began to gawk at her chest. It wasn't as if Janie was a triple D-cup, but she had enough to fill up an average sized male's mouth. Her mother always told her that more than a mouthful was simply too much.

Still, the way he stared at her breasts was rude and uncalled for; she would not take his forwardness without a challenge. "Hey, bub!" she called to him. "My eyes are up here."

Ethan was appalled. He had been caught staring at her shirt. Not only was the shirt a neon hot pink, which is what first caught his attention, but what kept him focused on it was the image. He asked, "I'm sorry. Is that a weight lifter on your shirt?"

Janie's hands were on her hips in defiance, "Yes, it is!"

He could not stop himself from frowning when he said, "The position and pose of the weightlifter implies that he is performing a dead overhead lift of your..."

"Again, my eyes are up here, Bub," she said.

Ethan could not let it go. He had never seen anything so blatantly sexist and sexy all in one neon hot pink package. The courage she had to wear it in public was one thing, but to wear to a meeting with the Mayor was another. She strolled past him into Mayor Galley's office, as pretty as she pleased, shaking the Mayor's hand and taking a seat.

Evidently, Ethan was the only person in the room who had not officially met the one and only Janie Cimoc. Neither the Mayor, the Deputy Mayor, nor the Mayor's assistant paid any attention to the tee. Ethan's eyes kept wandering back to it. There was even a weightlifting bar that sat perfectly under the two mounds, which held two black half circles that made it look as if her boobies were being cradled in the cups. The look on the weightlifter's face implied he was straining to hold up the two masses.

"I'm glad you are both here. I think once we finish this meeting we are going to have a great plan to save both of your businesses and the sanctity of our town," Mayor Galley Said. The rest of his team agreed with him.

Janie and Ethan spoke at the same time, "Our businesses are in trouble?"

The Mayor stood up and walked around his desk. He wore a long jacket that favored a tuxedo coat with tails. This jacket was complimentary to a pair of pin striped pants. To Ethan, the man looked like Mayor McCheese, bulbous nose included.

"The infidels are at the gate, and they are trying to destroy our way of life," the Mayor told them both. Through a series of rants filled with pontifications and lopsided allegories, the meeting boiled down to a big box bookstore coming to Venture.

"Ethan, my wife looks forward to book club at your store. I also send my assistant over every Thursday for a large cup of that Guatemala Huehuetenango. That is some mighty fine coffee there, my boy," the Mayor told him.

He turned his attention to Janie. "My kids have grown up in the Comic Book and your store is a staple in this town as well."

So that is who she is. Janie Cimoc. In the flesh.

Ethan spoke up, "Sir, I am not certain what this meeting is about. Can you please clarify why we are here?"

The Mayor looked at Ethan as if he had just burped up a bologna mouth fart. "That big box store is going to run you both out of business. You will be out of business in less than a year unless we can get ahead of those bastards!"

Janie spoke, "Sir, I am certain there is enough business for all three of us to survive."

"That is where you are wrong, Janie girl," Mayor Galley told her. He went on to explain that corporate stores like those bring in their own management teams. "Locals are only hired part time at best. The book prices are too high and what they give back to the community is minimal."

His eyes were filled with fire when he spoke to them,

"You two understand this town because you live here; you grew up here. Our way of life is about uplifting and supporting each other."

"What are you proposing, Mayor Galley?" Ethan asked.

Mayor Galley rubbed his rounded belly, "The city has two buildings, one on your side of town, Janie, and the other on your side, Ethan. The taxes are past due by three years, and now the properties belong to the City of Venture. I will let you have either building. You can pay up a year on the back taxes and set up a payment plan on the rest if you can't pay the taxes out right."

Janie was looking at Ethan and Ethan at her. She asked the same question of the Mayor that Ethan had, "What are you proposing, Mayor Galley?"

The Mayor seemed frustrated with them both. A large gust of coffee tinged breath came out of his mouth as he exhaled in exasperation. "In order for you two to be around after those corporate bastards come to town, you are going to have to combine forces!"

Ethan was staring at Janie's shirt. "She and I combine our businesses?"

"Son, until now, I had never thought you to be daft. I am starting to wonder," Mayor Galley said with a frown on his face.

"Your Honor," Ethan said as he rose, "I am not daft, nor short-sighted, but if I am given a choice on whether or not to combine my business with a random stranger, I would rather not!"

The mayor slammed his hand on the desk. "Fine! You will be out of business in less than a year. You too, Janie girl!"

He breathed deeply before waddling his way behind his

desk. "I am trying to do what is best for the two of you as well as the citizens of Venture. You two are young, and if you put your heads together, I am certain you can work out a fair deal and create the best of both worlds."

Mayor Galley opened his desk drawer and pulled out two sets of keys. "Here are the addresses and keys to both of the buildings. I need you two to make this work," he told them as he checked his watch.

Janie knew that meant their time was up. "Thank you, Mr. Mayor," she said as she led the way out to the office.

In the hallway, she faced Ethan. *My new business partner. He's kind of cute. Based on his slow-witted responses in the meeting, he doesn't seem very smart, though.*

Janie stuck out her small hand for a shake, "Put it there, part'nuh!"

Ethan's head was whirling. He accepted her handshake, then her business card that looked like a six-year-old had doodled stick people on a piece of card stock that was cut out at a whopside angel. Janie proceeded to rattle off a list of things she needed to get done by the end of the day.

Why is she telling me this?

"Call me later, after four, so we can decide to meet or ride together to look at those buildings tomorrow," she told him. He watched the neon pink shirt walk away. She was as interesting coming as she was going. On the back of the shirt was the same cartoon weightlifter, face down, doing pushups on dumbbells. The dumbbells were strategically placed on her butt cheeks. Each time she took a step, it looked as if the weightlifter was doing a one-armed press.

What just happened? Better yet, where in the hell did she

get that crazy ass shirt?

That, he would have to answer later. Right now, his mind was focused on his arms. The fine hairs were sticking up from all of the goose pimples that had arisen from when she shook his hand.

Ethan was about to start a new chapter in his book of life. There was a great deal of information that would need to be set up in order for the story to flow smoothly. If not, this story would end just like his last novel; a hot, flat, mess.

He was smiling when he got into his car.

I have goose bumps.

Chapter 4. Character Sketching…

It was a muggy afternoon when Ethan returned to his shop. His mother was engaged in a stimulating conversation with Dottie Meribodie about the book to be discussed in the non-fiction book club tonight. The book that the group had read was a memoir of an actress turned child advocate. In the conversation, Ethan overheard his mother mention how much the author had grown during the retelling of her journey from spoiled Hollywood royalty to helping her fellow man. Dottie chimed in, "She grew so much from page one to the end of the story. I felt taller by simply reading her words, like I had grown myself…"

Characters need growth.

Ethan ran into his office and pulled the manuscript from the bottom right drawer. Thumbing through the pages, he began to read. By the time he reached the end of Chapter 3, he knew what was wrong with the story. The story was not flat, the characters were. With the manuscript in his hand, he walked into the bookstore and watched the patrons milling about. Since it was book club night, there were at least 30 people in the store who normally only came for a cup of coffee or for book club meeting. If he didn't have the book clubs at the end of the month, the Mayor was correct; he would be out of business in less than a year.

I need growth.

Slowly, he made his way back into his office and called the woman from the meeting. *Janie. Now she seems like a real character.* It was a quick phone call, and he was set to head to her shop to take a look at her operation. His father,

Henry, walked in with a huge grin on his face.

Henry was beaming. "I heard you got called into the Mayor's office today!"

"Yes, but when I tell you why, you may not smile as much," Ethan spoke softly so his mother would not hear.

"Go ahead; pour me a cup of Joe first, then fill me in," Henry said.

As Ethan finished the conversation with the explanation, his father uttered some of his Southern ministerial sage words, "Before you climb in bed with a snake, you need to see how big his nest is." Henry's analogies were as bad as the Mayor's allegories.

That makes no sense.

"Son, what I am saying is…before you agree to go in to partnership with this woman, go and see how she conducts business," he said as he turned up the cup of coffee. Henry's eyes rolled up in his head. "This coffee is so good, I know it is a sin!"

"I should do that," Ethan responded.

"No, go do it now when she is least expecting you to show up. I will man the store here, start a fresh pot of this…delicious whatever fancy pants coffee this is," Henry said with his cheerful smile.

"Thanks, Dad."

Ethan left his store with one intention, to gain some understanding of the lady with the goofy shirt's business. She was the kind of character in a story that made a reader stay up at night to read one more paragraph. *Janie.* Never would he have imagined that he would leave his store with one idea in mind only to return refreshed with new ideas, new energy, and a new understanding of the importance of rich characters.

The Comic Book sat on the corner of Hattiesburg and Vine Streets in the lower income part of town. The homes were sturdy and old, and many had probably served as the servants' housing for the nicer homes a few blocks over. It was the East side of Venture. Good people lived here. People who worked hard, loved harder, and played the longest. A hippie commune used to be in that part of town as well, where many of the residents had a co-op of food and resources. Not many of the original inhabitants remained. The few who did were still very active in the community.

He watched for a while before deciding to venture inside. A cute young woman behind the counter greeted him as he walked in the door, "Welcome to the Comic Book!"

"Thanks," he mumbled as he worked his way around the store. Several of the comic books caught his eye as well as the brightly colored displays. Life-sized action figures were around the store, and a few patrons took selfies standing beside Thor or Captain America. Ethan took a mental picture as he moved on, milling about the establishment. *Where is that Janie?*

He heard her voice first. Then he spotted her. She had changed out of the neon pink tee to wear a new one that was equally as odd as the one she sported earlier. This shirt was baby blue with an image of atlas holding up the world. In this case, the world was her right boob.

Does she have a breast fixation?

"You know that's kind of pervy, right?" she asked him.

Ethan nearly jumped three feet in the air. He had completely zoned out while he tried to understand the psychology of why a woman would intentionally draw attention to her breasts. "I'm sorry. That is a very unique tee shirt; the one you had on earlier was as well," he said in his defense.

"Gee, thanks," Janie told him as she turned to greet an older lady with strawberry blonde hair. The woman looked like a reject from Woodstock. She wore a tie-dyed shirt over a blue cotton broom skirt with a pair of sandals that appeared to be made out of rags.

"I have cookies!" the lady said as she sat the tray on the counter. The instant she pulled back the cover, it was as if a cup of sugar was dropped at a picnic. Children began to materialize from everywhere like ants after having their sandy dirt pile bed disturbed. There were mini-vans unloading kids. There were station wagons, BMWs, Fords, Mercedes, and everything else imaginable, including bicycles that were left overturned by the door at ten minutes before six. A kid dressed like Sméagol slid in the door sideways, dragging his right foot. He reached up high on the counter, grabbed a cookie that he called 'my precious' and headed towards the rear of the store.

"Come have a look," Janie told him.

Ethan's eyes were wide when he saw a tabletop replica of Middle Earth in the corner of the room. Kids dressed like characters from Tolkien's tale began to reenact scenes. In the opposite corner, an older gentleman who looked like a bum began to read from the second book in the Tolkien series. He looked a great deal like a homeless Gandalf, but Janie stopped him from reading.

She asked him, "What is in the pipe, Gandalf?"

The old man hummed a familiar tune, trying to ignore her. She did not let it pass and told him "If I have told you once, I have told you twice, no smoking in here! You got it?"

"Aww, Janie. You can be such a stuffed shirt," the man told her.

"Stuffed shirt or not, I cannot have these kids leaving here smelling like cigarette smoke or whatever else you like puffing in that pipe," she said firmly.

The man was genuinely offended. "I mean really, Janie, if you keep treating me like this, I may have to stop coming around here to read to the kids," he said.

Janie walked over and hugged him. "I'm sorry, Daddy, but when your business revolves around other people's children, everything has be aboveboard."

"I know, Sweetie," he told her. He went back to his story. "Where was I...oh yes," he said and began to read again.

Ethan's face held no expression. Janie's, on the other hand, displayed a plethora of emotions. "At least this time the pipe has tobacco in it only," she said with some relief.

"Are you saying your father openly smokes ...other stuff?"

"Yes. He started growing it when he thought he had cancer," Janie told him.

"It's good to know that he has recovered and is in remission," he responded.

Janie stopped in the middle of the floor. "Remission? That man ain't never had no cancer. He just thought he did..."

"Whaaaa?" Ethan said, his mouth slightly open.

Her hands were perched on her hips. "Yes, my sister

brought home some non-organic mushrooms and canned tomato sauce to make pizzas. When he went the next morning, he had sinkers and not floaters so he thought she had infected him with '*the cancer*'," Janie said.

"Whaaaa?" Ethan said again. His brow crinkled in an attempt to understand what she meant.

"Oh, that's nothing. If I only had the time to tell you the one about him drinking a Coke…" she said. Her attention was drawn to the counter. The strawberry-haired woman was sitting there counting money.

"Mom, please count the money in the back room," she pleaded.

"That's your Mom?"

"Yes, we run a tight ship. That's my sister Meg," she said as she pointed to the girl behind the counter. "She and my brother Jem are the only paid employees other than me."

The doorbell jingled and in sauntered a short man in work coveralls. His hair, which was cut into a mullet, was greasy, his teeth were yellow, and his eyes went straight to Janie's shirt.

"I sure like that new shirt, Ms. Janie. Is that the one for this quarter?" he asked.

Janie was nicer to the man than Ethan thought she should have been, especially considering the way he was ogling her. The discomfort made Ethan feel protective and he stepped between her and the man.

This was not received pleasantly by Jimmy Earl. "Who 'dis man, Janie?"

Janie seemed very happy to share the news with her mother, Meg, and Jimmy Earl. "This is Ethan, my new business partner."

Chapter 5. Plotting away …

Jimmy Earl sat in the rear of the store with a comic book in his hand. He had eased his way from the merriment of the group to take note of the interactions between his Janie and the new man. From this vantage point, he had a clear view of the register and all the happy chatter and hand shaking taking place…with some dude. Some dude that would be working with his Janie. A black man that he immediately disliked, mainly because of the way Janie looked at him. She eyed him like he was some savior or something. *If she needs money for her business, I can give it to her. I can work some extra side jobs or something…*

"Jimmy Earl, what are you doing back in this corner?" Alice Cimoc asked him.

The man jumped as if someone had thrown firecrackers at his feet. He mumbled over his words while trying to steer clear of Janie's mom.

"I was just leaving, Ms. Alice. I don't want to get in the way of your celebrating and all," Jimmy Earl mumbled.

"Well, you have yourself a good evening," Alice told the odd little fellow as he slipped around the shelving and out the door.

Something about him made Alice very uncomfortable. This was also one of the reasons she was excited about Janie having a new partner, which would greatly cut down on the riff raff hanging around the store and around her daughter. Although Alice was proud of her daughter and the independence she displayed, she truly wanted her to get married. She noticed a spark between Ethan and Janie, but wasn't sure of what to make of it. Janie said they had only met earlier that day. Ethan seemed like a likable enough fellow to go into business with, but Alice wasn't sure it would be so easy to call him son-in-law. *Listen at me getting ahead of myself again.*

After Ethan left the shop, her parents hung back to help clean up. The clean-up times were instances her mother took advantage of by doling out her no-nonsense advice. A parataxis, one-sided conversation that really required no response from Janie, just a layering of clauses and phrases behind each other which would creep from her mother's disapproving lips.

"Janie. Sweetheart," Alice said. This made Janie cringe. *Those* two words. Two words that were followed by a string of layered phrases.

"You do know, don't you....that the eggs you were born with are the same number of eggs you will have all your life. Each year as you get older, so do those eggs. You cannot make a fresh omelet or bake a cake with old eggs. That cake will not rise and that omelet is going to taste funky," Alice informed her daughter.

Janie tried to remain respectful, "So Mom, are you implying that I find some rooster to fertilize my eggs?"

"Yes, Janie. Sweetheart. But it has to be a nice rooster that is going to build you a nice hen house to nurture those young chicks," Alice said with a smile. Janie wanted to fall out on the floor and pass out, especially when she turned around to find Ethan standing behind her.

"I thought you had left," she said softly.

"No, I forgot to set a time for you to come by my store and check out my shop tomorrow," he said with a twinkle in his eye. "I mean, I wouldn't want you to show up and catch me with all my eggs in one basket."

Janie's perfect peach skin began to warm from the base of her tee shirt to the roots of her hair, leaving bright red glowing circles on her cheeks.

"How does eleven sound, Ethan?" she asked flatly. Her breathing was unsteady as she watched the enjoyment of her discomfort radiate all over his face.

"That sounds like a good time. I'm an early riser, but I'm not up too bright or early with some of the roosters," he grinned at her.

She didn't know what came over her, but she picked up the nearest comic book from the shelf, rolled it up, and swatted him on the arm with it. Ethan was surprised at how playful she was with him.

"Janie, I'm sorry. I didn't mean to ruffle your feathers," he said while laughing. Alice placed her hand over her mouth to shield her smile when Janie swatted him again.

Ethan started to back up, which made Janie move forward, "Now Janie, we don't want to start off our business relationship on a bad note, running about like chickens with our heads cut off!"

That did it. Janie took off running after him and Ethan bolted for the front door. She stopped under the portico and stared at him as he scuttled off towards his car. Once inside the safety of his vehicle, he rolled by the doorway, grinning at her, "See you in the morning."

Instead of tooting his horn at her, he yelled out the window, "Bawk...bawk!"

Janie threw the comic book at the back of his car. Her cheeks were still rosy when she went back inside and Meg immediately made a comment.

"Janie, are you coming down with something? Your skin is all flushed and your arms are covered in goose pimples," Meg stated.

There was no real reason to answer her sister; she simply rubbed her skin, trying to press down the prickled flesh. Ethan Strom had just shown her a playful side of himself. *I can see working with him.*

It was unlike Ethan to be so nervous. He arrived at the shop a bit earlier than usual to ensure the shelves were straightened and there was no dust about. Oddly enough, he wanted to impress Janie and come across as a solid business partner. In her shop, he noticed several things which were lacking in his own, mainly so many children and teens. Even when he booked a semi-famous Georgia best-selling children's author, he still did not have the turnout she received on her Wednesday game night. The children dressing up as their favorite characters was cool. Once he counted the $5 per head for 25 kids that were present, if she did those numbers each week, the Comic Book pulled in roughly three grand a month, just in kids hanging out. A larger store would make a world of difference, especially if Middle Earth went from a tabletop to a floor map.

A floor map projected onto the floor.

A floor map with changeable landscapes.

A floor map that could rotate each week as the battle moved through the lands of Middle Earth.

He jotted down this idea in a new notebook. His mood was light as he began the Thursday brew of Guatemala Huehuetenango. As soon as the carafe was full, the doorbell chimed and instead of the Mayor's assistant, the man himself walked into the door, a giant coffee mug in hand, a smile on his face, and questions on the top of his mind.

"Ethan, my boy, I hope you have taken into consideration our conversation from yesterday. I firmly believe that if you and Janie put your minds together that you can create something unique for this community," he told him.

"I think you are right, Mayor Galley," Ethan told him as he emptied the whole pot of coffee, sans one cupful, into the man's mug.

"Good; I look forward to seeing what you two come up with," the Mayor told him as he handed him a twenty for the coffee and waddled his way to the door.

It was Thriller Thursday and thus far the month had shaped up well. Before he could get the second pot of coffee finished, four other people showed up to buy a cup and also overpaid. By the time 11 am rolled around, he was in a really great mood. It only got better when Janie arrived.

In his head were all of these ideas. Possibilities for a new shop, a new vision; he was plotting away on paper, but when he looked up and saw her, everything in his mind changed. The ideas transformed even more after he had a conversation with the free spirit that was Janie Cimoc.

Chapter 6. Creating a Dialogue...

He knew Janie had entered Bartleby's simply by the customers' reactions. Based on the responses, he knew she was wearing another one of those goofy tee shirts that brought attention to her ladies. It immediately caught his eye because this one was actually funny.

The tee was neon green with bold navy letters and read: *Hot Boiled Peanuts*. It had half an open peanut shell whose placement cradled her boobies with a three dimensional thermometer sticking up from her left boob with 98.6° emboldened on the scale. His hand covered his mouth to stifle his laughter when old Mrs. Murphy eyeballed the shirt with her one good eye and proceeded to clutch her pearls in offense.

"Hey there, Pat'nuh!" she said as she walked over to him. To his shock, she didn't shake his hand but embraced him full on with a giant hug that rendered feelings of squishiness that a body might have after receiving a kiss from a unicorn.

The smile was genuine as he asked, "Would you like a cup of coffee?"

"Nah, I don't do caffeine; it makes me twitchy," she told him.

"Come on in my office," he said to her. His fingers waved at the young lady who walked behind the counter to cover for him. "Janie, would you like some tea instead?"

"Yes, that would be nice," she told him. He nodded to the young lady behind the counter to bring Janie a cup.

Janie followed him into a very neat but really masculine office that was filled with the scent of man. *Ethan's scent.* She stared at the wall for a second, allowing her eyes to adjust. The smell of the room made her pupils dilate. It was so manly. It held earthy undertones from his soap with a faint scent of sweat. Her belly felt as if her eggs were also twitching and ready to be released for fertilization. Before her body could embarrass her even more, the young lady from the counter brought her in a cup of tea along with a small tray of deviled and pickled eggs.

The twinkle in his eye was unmistakable when he offered her a snack. Janie didn't bite as she kicked off her well-worn Birkenstocks to fold her knees into the chair under her body lotus style. Ethan had never seen a woman sit like that in public, let alone in a skirt. A skirt that he could see under. He shifted his position in his chair so that his view was now obstructed. *Focus Ethan.*

"You are really different," Ethan said as he watched her use a napkin to pick up one of the deviled eggs.

"And you are a busted comedian. The eggs are funny, but Janie is hungry, so Janie is going to eat the food put before her," she said as she stuffed an egg in her mouth.

Ethan's brow was furrowed as he looked at her with more than a mild curiosity. "Do you often refer to yourself in third person?"

"Only when the voice of reason needs to speak on my behalf instead of me saying what is actually on my mind. I mean, for all you know, that whole egg thing with my mom could be a point of contention for me, yet you mock me, poking fun at my expense. I really should blast you, but you were considerate to bring food for our meeting. That I am thankful for and accept." She ate another egg, washed it down with tea, and sucked her front teeth to make sure nothing was caught in between. To make certain no remnants hovered between the crevices, she gave a dental flash of her pearlies to Ethan, asking him to check her teeth to make sure the coast was clear.

He nodded his head to let her know there were no stragglers hanging about in the cracks of her teeth. "I'm sorry; I meant no offense," he said.

"...And obviously I took none as I ate your smelly deviled eggs," she said with raised brows.

As he was about to change the subject to focus on business, a familiar voice could be heard in the bookstore. It was loud. It was brash. It was Kate. She was yelling at Marta, the young lady working the counter.

"I know he is here; he is always here," she yelled at the girl. "I will show myself to his office!"

And she did. The door was open when she bounded around the corner. Her eyes immediately rested on Janie. Eyes that were filled with fire, venom, and the full weighted anger of 135 pounds of pissed off black woman. Janie unfolded her legs as her feet slipped into her shoes. Janie was smirking at Ethan, shaking her head, and said, "Uhmmm....Janie is going to take her eggs and this tea and wait for you in the other room."

She grabbed the plate of eggs, scooting around Kate, careful to stay clear as she made her way out the door.

"Did you dump me for Cinderella? Please tell me you didn't do something so cliché as leave me for a white woman?" Kate asked with her hands on her hips.

"I didn't dump you. We just don't want the same things, so I freed you up to find someone who wanted what you wanted," he told her. "I'm not certain how that makes me the bad guy in this scenario. You issued an ultimatum, I responded."

Kate was angry. Her words were worse as she spat

them at Ethan. "You're the bad guy because your high yella ass is further polluting our race by mixing it up with some trailer park trollop. What's so special about her? Can she suck the shine off a door knob?"

The look of disgust on Ethan's face made Kate back up. "Janie is the owner of the Comic Book. I am not dating her and you will apologize this instant for referring to her in such a degrading manner."

"I will do no such thing!" Kate said with defiance.

"...And I have no desire to ever see your face again. Please leave right now and do not come back," Ethan told her.

Kate was stunned.

She was angry.

She was hurt.

This inner rage helped fuel an even bigger bonfire when she and Ethan left his office to walk into the bookstore and find Janie with Hester. The two ladies stood in an embrace. What drew Ethan's eyes to the women was his mother. She was hugging Janie with her eyes closed. *That… is an intimate moment.*

Kate was furious. In her wrath, she attempted to push a stack of books off a table, but only succeed in bruising her arm. "Great! Just flippin' great! She's your business partner, my ass!"

Hester and Janie watched in amusement. Janie's mouth was twisted to the side when she whispered to Hester using her third person self-muting button, "Janie is not nosey, but we take it that Ethan recently broke up with the angry black lady?"

Not missing a beat, Hester responded in the same muted fashion, referring to her role in her son's life in third person as well, "Yes, and Momma was truly happy about it."

Janie held out her hand for a down low fist bump. Hester met her halfway, bumping fists in an unseen solidarity.

Ethan walked over to join them. "I'm glad to see you two have met," he said as he watched Kate leave the store.

"Oh!" Janie said suddenly. She wore a bright purple sling hobo bag which appeared to wrap around her small frame. A matching purple string tied together her blond ponytail that fell down her back between her shoulder blades. "I brought you something," she told him with pride.

From the bag she pulled out a black tee shirt, handing it to him with a large grin. Her smile got even larger as he unfurled the cotton to hold it up to read it. Ethan was careful to hold it at an angle away from his mother's eyes just in case it was along the same lines as the tee shirts Janie seemed to enjoy wearing. Her gift to him was far worse than the three he had seen her wear. The peanut one she wore today was really over the top, but this may have taken the cake. It read *"I like to conjugate my dangling participle."*

Ethan's face was deadpan as he looked at Janie.

Janie was brimming with pride like a cat that had just brought him a half-dead convulsing bird. Her eyes were searching his for acknowledgement that this gift she presented meant something to her thereby connoting a meaning for him as well. For that reason, he made a point to not hurt her feelings, but he sure as hell would never be caught dead or alive wearing that damned shirt.

"Thank you, Janie," he said with a forced smile.

Hester wanted to see the shirt. Ethan tried to hide the

offensive fabric behind his back, but she gave him that Momma look and he handed it over. His mother held up the tee and read it. After she read it she noticed the shirt Janie was wearing.

"Oh my Jesus," she said softly. Hester passed the shirt back to Ethan and headed to the counter to get her coffee. Over her shoulder she sweetly added, "Nice meeting you, Janie.'

"Your Mom is cool people," Janie said.

"Thanks," he mumbled. His mother had most likely never in her life been labeled as cool, probably not even by the kids she hung out with in high school. Yet, Janie saw something in his mother few people did—an acceptance of her as she stood. Unlike Kate who immediately made a snap judgment, his mother took Janie at face value, which did make her a cool person.

Janie is unquestionably a dynamic character.

It was definitely going to be interesting partnering with her because he was certain there was never going to be a dull moment.

Chapter 7. Revising the Plot...

If there was a means to record the first full day which Ethan Strom spent in Janie's company, it would have certainly gotten two million hits on a video streaming website. It could easily be stated that he entered the seven stages of grief in less than eight hours and ended the day resigned in the acceptance that Janie was probably going to drive him insane. He could not stop grinning at the thought of it because the more time he spent with her, the more he liked the odd woman.

Saturday was crisp and clear for a May morning as he drove his very clean Ford to the Comic Book. Uncertain where she lived and afraid to ask for fear of being considered nosey, he agreed to meet her at the shop. She bounded out of the front door, fresh faced, wearing a giant grin, and ready to look at some buildings. Instead of her purple hobo bag, she carried a knapsack loaded with supplies, everything from wet wipes to flashlights, but the first thing Ethan noticed were her feet. Janie was still wearing those ratty Birkenstocks.

"Those shoes may not be the best choice," he told her as she slid into the passenger seat. This was the second time he noticed her scent. It was something faint and sweet. He couldn't place his finger on top of it, but it was familiar to him.

"Well, if I had another pair of shoes, I would have them on, Ethan."

"Then, we will need to stop and buy you a pair, Janie," he said back in the same tone she had spoken to him.

"If I had money to buy another pair, Ethan, this

conversation would not be necessary, now would it?" Her head was cocked to the side as she spoke to him.

Before entering into this partnership, a great number of factors would have to be considered. He would not agree to this merger until he saw her books, but an idea for the combined stores was fueling him to press forward, like some outdated homing beacon beckoning him to roost.

As he turned down Elmherst Avenue, he spotted the sign for a discount family department store. In his head, they could pick her up a pair of covered shoes for less than $20. They only needed to run in the store, try on some shoes, buy the pair, and continue on with their day.

It wasn't that simple. Ethan noticed her tee shirt. This bright red one read: *These are ma' fun bags*. He didn't want to go into a family store with her wearing that shirt.

"Where do you get all of these provocative shirts?" he asked because he truly wanted to know.

"My sister Meg and I design them. We are hoping to launch our website later this year. Right now we are only selling ones and twosies, but I know we are on to something here." She started toward the door, but he touched her arm.

Ethan tried to gather his thoughts before he said anything else to her, "Uhmm...they are very...uhmmm....titillating...?" He knew immediately after saying it that the wrong word had been used.

"Why? Because it draws attention to my boobs?" Janie asked him.

His lips were pressed tightly together. "Yes...Janie, it's not appropriate!"

Janie turned so slowly that Ethan held his breath in anticipation of the verbal ass whipping she was about to unleash on him.

"They are just titties, Ethan. You do know your mother has a pair," she said softly.

Ethan opened his mouth, but gave it a second thought and opted instead to shut up. Janie, unfortunately, had no intention of doing so until she made sure he understood where she stood.

"Based on the closeness between you and your mother, I would hazard a guess that she fed you from her breast," she said. "Is your mother still married to your father?"

"She is," he answered, hesitant to know where she was heading next.

"I'm sure in the privacy of their home, your daddy considers those boobies to be his fun bags," she said. She moved two steps closer to him. "Do you have a sister?"

Ethan didn't like where this was going. "Yes, I do, Janie."

"Well, guess what, she has a set of titties too, Ethan!" Janie watched him gnawing on his lip. "If she is married or seeing someone, they too are probably playing with your sister's fun bags!"

He was shaking his head, trying to walk away from her. Janie got loud, "Oh, don't try to walk away from Janie now, Mr. Appropriate. Because you are worried Janie is going to ask how much you like to juggle a pair of fun bags. Is that it, Ethan? Are you a titty man?"

The face which stared her down was serious. "Stop it right now. You will not embarrass me in public with this vulgarity! I asked you a simple question. Nothing more. Nothing less," he said with anger in his voice. His words were powerful. He used a commanding tone. He somehow seemed...taller. *Oooh, Janie likes.*

"I'm sorry," Janie said. "I just get so sick of men trying to dictate to women what we can or should wear. There are a-holes sitting in legislation in Atlanta passing laws and edicts about my reproductive rights all the while sliding into bed with some shady pharmaceutical company who is buying up placenta and feeding it back to young women in their drugs and shampoo. They have convinced young women to stick on a patch that allows their bodies to self-cleanse only once a year, and they call it progress. I call it oppression. These are my titties. This is my body. If anyone is going to profit off of it, it will be me."

Ethan watched her face closely. She was a passionate creature. An enigma of a woman. Before he could respond, a young lady passed by and read her shirt.

"Cool, where can I get one of those?" The red head asked.

Janie handed the girl one of her business cards with the stick figure people on it. "You can call and place your order or drop by the store and peruse our catalog," she told the lady who walked away happy.

Ethan's mouth dropped, "You have a catalog?"

"Not really," she whispered. "It is a three-ringed binder with trading card sheets along with trading card-sized designs in it."

He started laughing.

"Hey, you gotta start somewhere," she told him.

What can I say? "Well, let's go inside and start by getting Janie a pair of shoes," he responded.

It seemed so natural for her as she linked her arm into his, almost skipping like a kid going to get new school clothes. "Janie would like that a whole lot," she said with a giant grin.

She would not let the opportunity to learn more about Ethan pass. She asked him softly, "So Ethan, are you a breast man?"

He said nothing as he continued to walk. She was grinning at him like he was about to buy her the first ice cream cone of the summer season when she asked, "So you are not going to answer my question?"

"I would rather not!"

Her bottom lip was poked out and quivering. He looked down at her face, avoiding visual contact with her fun bags. "Yes I am, Janie."

"I knew it!" She said nothing more, but in her mind she was happy, because Janie liked that idea a whole lot as well. More so the idea of Ethan using his forceful voice while he played with her bags of fun appealed to her a bit more than it should have.

Jimmy Earl, who sat in the passenger seat of the car in the parking lot watching the two, did not like anything he was seeing. He did not like it in the least. She was his Janie. His alone. He only needed to find a way to remind her of his undying love. Then the fancy black man would go away and leave them in peace.

Even if he had to make him.

Chapter 8. Ship, shape, and scratch that…

It did not take long to locate a sturdy pair of work shoes. Janie, of course, picked boots that were pink. Neither of them thought about bringing a pair of socks, so Ethan purchased a few sets of those as well. He reached for the solid pair that would provide the most comfort while she broke in the work boots, and Janie grabbed a duo of multi-colored striped socks with little toes for her little toes.

"These are sooooo cute and fun. Can I have these, Ethan?" She was so excited he could not bring himself to say no. He still erred on the side of caution and purchased the functional pairs as well.

Janie was different from any woman he had ever been around. Things that she ogled in the store, most of the women he knew would not want to purchase from this chain, but buy them somewhere a tad bit more upscale, simply because of the quality. One of the items he caught her staring at for a while was a blue dress.

"Do they have it in your size?" He asked.

She was embarrassed for even looking. *Janie girl, you have too many priorities to even look at that thing.* "Rarely do these types of stores carry my size. I'm a size eight. Most of these stores carry larger sizes and just kids. When something does come in my size, it's gone fast!"

That was the last thing said on the subject. "Oh, Ethan, I do need the receipt so I can reimburse you at the end of the month."

"Consider it my gift to you," he told her.

"Nope. We cannot start off this relationship with you buying Janie things and Janie not paying you back. That is not good business. And it is not something we want to practice," she said.

"Fair enough," he said and handed her the receipt for $27.36.

"You will get this back," she told him firmly.

He had no doubt that she would honor her words. His trust in her was beginning to grow.

Janie stood in front of the building on Waterston Street eyeing the dilapidated structure with boarded up windows over burglar bars.

"That is not a good sign," he told her.

"This place is a pile of shit," she said flatly.

"We can't discount it without giving a good look inside. It may be a solid ship, and we just need to make her seaworthy. The back taxes are only three grand, and paying the city wouldn't be a struggle," he told her.

"Yes, but paying the three hundred grand to contractors to redo the wiring that the mice have gnawed through or to remove the asbestos and black mold will be," she told him. "They have boarded windows over burglar bars, which means it was probably robbed often before they closed shop."

"Good point," he told her.

She walked around the side of the building, throwing her hands up in exasperation.

"What is the point of boarded windows when the building has a giant hole in the side of it?" Janie didn't give him a chance to answer; she had already walked back to the car.

Ethan walked the full building, seeing what else was visibly wrong. There was a lot. This one was not an option. The Mayor had called him yesterday to add one more building to the list, so he and Janie headed to that one next.

She hated that one as well. "My parents have a co-op three blocks over and I grew up in this neighborhood. Any money that was in this community moved out long ago; my parents' business is proof of the reason not to choose this one, so scratch it, too."

"We can't simply say no; the last one may be worse than all three. You have to keep an open mind. It will take a combined vision on both our parts to pull this together," he told her.

Janie rode in silence while they made their way across town. As if she suddenly remembered something, she turned in the seat. The leather squeaked under her weight as she faced him in the car. "Ethan, I bet you went to college."

"I did," he told her.

"I never had a chance," she said softly. Her blond head turned to stare out the window. "I was thinking, I could close the shop and go to school full time."

"Is that what you would like to do Janie?"

"I think about it sometimes. You know, I am approaching 27, and my eggs are getting older, too…"

A hand, calm, manicured, and callous free, reached over to touch hers, gently stroking the skin. "I do believe this last building will tell us exactly what we should do next," Ethan told her.

"The first one was awful. The second one didn't fit our needs. It's optimistic to assume the last one will be just right. I'm too damned old to be Goldilocks or to believe in fairytales, Ethan, but as you asked, I shall keep an open mind," she told him.

The GPS voice sounded louder than normal as it issued instructions, "Turn right on Baker Street. In point five miles, turn left on Butcher Street." Ethan followed the instructions as the voice came across the speakers once more. "Turn right onto Candlestick; your destination is on the left."

Both Ethan and Janie were leaning forward in their seats in anticipation. "You have arrived at your destination," said the voice through the speakers.

It was the old Roxy Music Hall and Theater. The building was located in a very active part of town where many old family owned businesses still operated and thrived. The marquee above the building still said Roxy, but many of the lights were burned out or missing. Janie noticed immediately the second floor and the large windows. *Upstairs apartments; I hope they are in good shape.*

Ethan's mind rested upon the poster holders. *Those would be perfect for upcoming events.*

They were both fumbling, trying to grab their flashlights as well as the keys. The paint was peeling on the outside of the wooden frame of the building and the brass door holders had patina, but the outside had some charm.

"A couple of bistro sets out front for the coffee crowd..." Ethan said.

"A couple of urns with fresh seasonal plants..." she replied.

The glass in the front door was still intact. The side

display windows were charming and Ethan thought about the comic book figures that could stand in one while the latest best seller could be featured in the other. He inserted the key in the lock and heard the tumblers give away for entrance. The doorbell jangled overhead as he and Janie entered, arm in arm, nervous, excited and brimming with anticipation. The flashlights clicked on and the beams of light sprayed around the space.

"Hello..." Janie called into the darkness.

"If someone answers you back, you are on your own. I will leave your ass in here," Ethan told her. "You will be running down the street behind the car yelling, 'Wait for me, Ethan. Janie don't want to stay here!'"

Janie tilted the flashlight to shine upon her face like a storyteller around a campfire. "Again, you are a busted comedian. That is not funny. Besides...."

She turned the light towards where she thought a window would be. "...I would trip you up and run up your back to get out of here first!"

Her flashlight was smaller than his. "Ethan, yours is bigger, can you shine some of that light over here, please," she told him as she pulled the heavy brocaded drapery back allowing light to flood into the space. Both she and Ethan's breath caught.

From the hardwood floors to the balconies and the performance stage, it was evident what they both were thinking. "Home," they said at the same time.

For a mere $4,600 in back taxes, the outdated building in the center of Candlestick Street would be the new location for their bookstore.

Ethan looked at her. "I think we should keep the original name..."

"...And we call it the Roxy," she finished his sentence.

Ethan only nodded as he pulled her into his arms. He didn't know why he was hugging her; it simply felt natural. It must have felt that way to her as well. Janie hugged him back, pleased, and they stood together like a young couple finding their first home.

Outside on the street, a set of eyes watched the pair. Anger simmered in a large cauldron of contempt like a meal for the Witches of Weird. Anyone observing the young pair could see they were indeed a new couple, starting something fresh in their lives. The hostile eyes that watched were not going to allow any of their dreams to come to fruition. There was no way these two were going to start something new without first having a reckoning with the old.

Chapter 9. Throwing in some conflict...

Ethan didn't want to chance looking about the space any longer without some power, a long stick, and something to serve as protection. It was nearly one and Janie's stomach was growling. Loudly.

"There's a little restaurant across the way. Let me treat you to lunch," he told her.

"I brought a few sandwiches if you want one," she told him.

"No, we are celebrating. There is a great deal to discuss, plan, and strategize over this new space. I have a vision, but I want to hear yours. Then we combine the two and we move forward," he told her. "I mean, if you still want to move forward with me?"

It wasn't the question that he posed to her which made her pause and her pulse race, but the tone in which he posed the question.

"Yes, Ethan, I would like to move forward with you," she responded. Her hand found his as he locked the door, and they headed across the street to the quaint bistro. Ethan also needed to see if his coffee business was going to disturb anyone else's before he cranked up that beautiful antique copper coffee maker.

The eatery was a quaint little dine-in with a modest lunch fare and only ten tables. It was obviously a Mom & Pop shop that was most likely operated by one of the owner's kids. A thirty-something-year-old brunette came from the back to bring out some menus.

She spoke to them as if they were old friends, "Hey there, guys; I just made some fresh chicken salad a little while ago, or if you want to go with a BLT or a burger and fries, I can cook it up for you," she said.

Ethan asked, "The chicken salad sounds good to me. What are you having, Janie?"

It had been such a long time since she had beef that a juicy burger and fries sounded like manna from Heaven. "I'll take that burger and throw some bacon on top of it with those fried taters," Janie said with a huge grin.

"What do you guys want to drink?" the waitress asked. "I have some sweet tea I just brewed as well as some fresh squeezed lemonade."

"I'll take the lemonade," Ethan said.

Janie opted for nothing. Not even a bottle of water. She scoffed at his suggestion, "Seriously Ethan, bottled water is nothing more than tap water they heated and ran through reverse osmosis. It's the plastic that will get you in the end. All those free radicals slowly eating away at you..." Her eyes were squinted as she emphasized her words.

He shook his head in disbelief. "You are a conundrum ..."

The waitress returned to the table with the drink order. "I'm Bitsy. I own the place. I saw you guys looking at the old theater across the street."

"Yes, we are looking at moving our book store there," Janie spoke to the woman, her body language asking the woman to divulge secrets about the neighborhood, and Bitsy complied. The woman opened her mouth and told the whole kit and caboodle she held in her head. In less than three minutes, they had everything they needed to know about peak times, traffic flow, and what their bookstore would mean to the area. It was also then that Ethan and

Janie found out that Bitsy was the Mayor's little sister.

She hadn't even walked away from the table to fetch their order when Kate walked in, still angry and filled to the brim with piss mixed with vinegar. *Did she follow us?* She spotted them and opened her mouth to start in on Ethan. But Janie was hungry and fixated on that burger; there was no way she was going to allow this woman to ruin the first decent meal she'd get to enjoy in months.

Before the first syllable rolled between Kate's lips, Janie held up her hand, "Thank you for letting me know. Now I have to find out for myself."

Kate words were lodged in her throat as she stared at Janie. *I haven't said anything. Letting her know what?*

As if she'd read Kate's thought, she continued talking. "I mean honestly, I just met this man a few days ago and until this minute, I had no interest in sleeping with him. Thanks to you, now I do." Janie said.

It was hard for Kate to grasp what Janie was saying, leaving Janie to break it down for her. "Seriously, this man must be hell in bed for you to follow him about and be this angry that you can't have any more of his loving. Shit...you have gone in to full-blown stalker mode, embarrassing yourself like this...," Janie looked Ethan squarely in his eyes, "I am going to have to try some of that out."

Ethan's face was flat. It was hard for him not to react. Even more so when Janie said, "I am sorry Ethan, but you are going to have to put out."

His facial expression did not change. "When you put it like that, I guess I may have to...I understand; inquiring minds need answers."

"We will come up with a safe word so we don't hurt each other, but I want you to double down on whatever you put on her. I want your A-game times two," Janie said calmly.

She treated Kate as if she were not even standing next to the table with her fists balled up. Janie was mentally daring the woman to hit her, but mainly, her mind was on that burger. She smiled at Ethan when she said, "Oh, here comes our food."

Kate was still standing at the table: hurt, more confused, and outdone. Ethan looked up at her. "I'm sorry Kate. I don't mean to be rude, but we are about to have lunch; did you need to speak with me about something?"

Janie didn't give her a chance to respond as she reached across the table to grab Ethan's hand and said, "Bless the food Ethan, please." Again, dismissing Kate.

They lowered their heads as Kate stormed out the door fuming, "You two are assholes. You deserve each other!"

To Janie, the woman was irrelevant. Her whole focus had now changed about her new partner. Although she said it in a spirited tone, her intentions were anything but playful. Quiet men who were often so reserved in their daily lives could be freaks in the bedroom. At least that is what her friends told her.

Thus far, her life had been anything but filled with romance, courtship, and love. The one time she tried to date, the boy made a fool out her and she swore off men. A year or so ago, she tried a woman and that was awkward, weird, and unsatisfying.

Ethan looked as if he could get the job done. Based on how Kate was reacting, he must be a very skilled lover. *Lover. Janie likes the sound of that word.* She bit into her burger and grinned at him.

He watched her eat like she had not been fed in a month. He ordered another burger to go for her, and something odd settled into his chest. There was a great deal more to Janie's life and he found himself wanting to know about it all. Moreover, the words she had uttered to Kate had truth in them that she had not tried to hide.

Ethan didn't think that Janie knew how to hide anything, least of all her emotions. For some odd reason, it was comforting to know his new partner was transparent. He was now starting to wish he had been the same way with Kate. She was hurting and felt as if he betrayed her, but he hadn't. At some point, he would help her understand that. Right now, his attention was solely for two other ladies in his life, The Roxy and the enigma called Janie Cimoc.

Chapter 10. Creating the Outline...

The Reverend Henry Strom stood tall in the pulpit while he delivered his Sunday morning sermon to his congregation of two hundred and fifty. Heads swayed in the pews as the choir hummed behind the fever-pitched cadence of the closing sermon for which Henry was well known. He often told his son that he was not going to have his members leave on Sunday with a pocketful of crumbs, but he would send them forward into the week with a loaf of bread.

"As you go forward into your week, it is easy to understand how you are living your life, but as a servant, it is importunate that you recognize how others may be living theirs as well," Henry said to the crowd.

When Ethan rose from the pew, he felt full and fortified. More than that, a new sense of purpose filled his soul. Each Sunday after service, his parents either went to the all you can eat Chinese buffet or the all you could eat salt fest at the other food trough in town.

"Ethan, are you joining us today for lunch?" Hester wanted to know.

"I actually have a few things I need to get done before this evening," he replied.

Hester moved closer to pick a piece of lint from his necktie. "You have plans with that cute little Janie?"

Henry, totally engrossed in loading the back seat of his 2000 Cadillac Brougham with goodies for the senior home he would visit after they had lunch, looked up at his son. "Who is Janie? Have I met her?" Henry wanted to know.

"No, Dad, once you meet Janie, you will never forget

her," he said with a half-smile.

"It seems she has really made an impression on you, son." He watched the twinkling in Ethan's eyes.

Ethan acknowledged his father's words, but today he planned to implement the ones Henry spoke in the sermon. Janie had only been in his life for a few days but it seemed more like each day equated a year. *Five days.*

In five days, Janie had made him more hopeful about his life and the future of his business than the eight years he had spent building it. He pulled out the wacky business card she had given him and dialed the number.

Janie answered his call on the second ring, "The Comic Book; this is Janie."

The melody of her voice reminded him of the first rainbow after a summer shower, bright, colorful, and filled with promise. Ethan said, "Hello, Janie; this is Ethan. I was wondering if you were free this evening to discuss some details of our upcoming merger."

She heard a loud bump in the back of the store and she was distracted momentarily before she responded. Honestly, she wasn't certain if his request was a double entendre or if he actually wanted to discuss the businesses.

"Do you mean of our businesses or our bodies?" she asked.

"The businesses, Janie. I was hoping you were free for dinner," he said.

Ethan checked his watch; it was already three in the afternoon. "Can I pick you up at five?"

"As long as there is food involved, it sounds good to me," she replied and she hung up the phone.

Where the hell does she live? Ethan dialed her number once more. Again she answered on the second ring, "The

Comic Book; this is Janie."

"It would help if I knew where you lived so I can know where to pick you up." Ethan said slowly.

"Stop being silly; I'm at the shop. The shop closes at five. Pick me up from the shop," she told him.

"Oh, well okay," he said into the line.

She hung up again.

What the hell is wrong with this woman?

Several ideas came to him at once. The first was where he wanted to take her to dinner. The second was that she would probably wear a stupid tee shirt that would not allow them entrance into the restaurant. The third idea that came in his head he liked a whole lot more than first two ideas. *If you don't like something, change it.*

It had been a while since he had been shopping, especially for a woman. Buying for women in his world usually meant gift cards for the holidays and flowers for birthdays. One year, he had saved and bought his sister a stethoscope for Christmas when he learned she wanted to be a doctor. Other than that, he would pick the appropriate gift card or flowers that fit the occasion.

The sun beamed down on his head, adding more heat to his already sweating scalp. He didn't know how Janie was going to react to this, but it felt right to him, so he was going to go for it. He crossed the parking lot and entered the Old Navy store. There was still a coupon in his car from the mail he brought in the other day, which is what made him come here to find her something. A bubbly young teen met him at the door.

"If you need any help finding something, let me know," she said.

Ethan jumped on the request. "Yes, I want a casual

dress for an adult woman, size 8 and in pink," he said.

He followed her to the rack of dresses, but he saw a multi-colored one with purple and blues that would look really lovely on Janie. "I want that one," he said. "I also need a pair of shoes," he said. He thought about the boots and the size they had purchased. "Those should be in a size 7."

Satisfied with his choices, he made his way to the register. A few hair bows, ribbons, and clips were available and he grabbed a purple one with feathers, along with a blue faux leather bag. He actually found himself humming as he made his way to the car and drove to her shop.

He arrived to find the weird guy with the dirty mullet hanging around the front door peering in. Ethan spoke to the man as he stepped around him to enter the Comic Book. Meg was behind the counter wearing a yellow tee that read: *Hey, the size of these does not match my I.Q.*

To his surprise, Janie was wearing jeans and a plain tee. No words on the front. A sense of relief fell over him until she turned around to pick up a box of comics from under the display table. The back of the shirt read: *It's an ass. Your mama has one, too.*

Thank God for forethought. His hand tightened around the bag.

"Oh hey, Ethan! I didn't know you were here," she said with a grin as she came over to hug him.

Janie felt warm in his arms. *Strawberries.*

The smell was strawberries and peaches.

Her hair smelled like a fresh fruit salad, and he held her longer than he should have, which was noticed by both Meg and Janie. Especially when he realized he was hugging her with his eyes closed.

Meg, unfiltered like her big sister, said, "Get a room!"

Janie pulled away laughing. "Hugs like that, hell, I may start stalking you too!" He didn't respond; she didn't give him time. "Hey, what's in the bag?"

Like a giant oaf, he stuck the bag out in front of him like a kid handing a girl his favorite pet frog. "This is for you," he said sheepishly. His cheeks were red as he blushed uncomfortably.

Janie peered inside the bag to see the shoes and the dress.

"You bought me a dress and shoes?" Her brow was crinkled.

"Yes, for you to wear to dinner tonight. I thought the dress was pretty and would look lovely on you. I bought the shoes and bag because it is how my sister and mom shop..."

Janie's facial expression remained stoic as she pulled the dress from the bag. Meg didn't hide her excitement as she fussed and oohed over the items.

"Go change, Janie. You are going to look so amazing in that dress," Meg fawned.

But Janie hadn't moved.

"Were you worried I was going to wear something to embarrass you?" she asked him.

Ethan moved closer to push a blond tendril behind her ear. "No, I wanted to take you out to dinner and make every man in the room wish he was me."

There was no mistaking the look she gave him. It was the second time Janie looked at him like a woman looks at her man.

Ethan liked it.

He liked it a whole lot.

Chapter 11. Adding More Character...

The young man appeared from out of nowhere. Meg seemed very comfortable with him and based on the strawberry blond hair, Ethan assumed he was their brother. His eyes were fixed on Ethan as he moved toward the front of the store to stand toe to toe with him. Holden said nothing as he took Ethan in from head to toe with an unwavering gaze.

Holden spoke slowly with a lazy Southern drawl that none of the other family members possessed. His eyes were focused in on Ethan's. "Day six...and you show up with clothes and shoes..."

"Janie works hard plus there are a lot of details we have to iron out in a short period of time, so I thought it would be nice to take her to dinner," Ethan told him.

"Be wary of the man who bears gifts," Holden said. The man had not moved an inch from where he stopped on the floor.

Ethan maintained his ground. "She and I are going to be partners. Plus, I thought the dress was bright and colorful; I thought she would like it."

"I can't respect a man I don't trust," Holden said.

"And I can't trust a man I don't respect," Ethan responded.

Neither man moved. Yet Ethan reluctantly backed down. "I get it. I have a sister, I know how you feel."

"No. You. Don't." Holden said.

This was not working. Ethan needed a new tactic. "I'm going to be her business partner. My business and livelihood is going to be tied to your sister. The happier I can make her, the better our business will be."

"Yes, that may be true, but you can't buy her or force her happiness with pretty dresses and pink boots," Holden said.

He watched Holden closely. It was Ethan's turn to take him all in. He couldn't be any more than twenty-five years old, but like Janie, he had old eyes. Holden sported a neatly trimmed goatee and long hair that he had tied back into a ponytail. By looking at his arms and hands, Ethan knew he had a trade job.

"My name is Ethan. Ethan Strom," he told.

"I'm Holden," he said.

"Holden, what can I do or say to earn your trust?" he asked.

"You can start by being honest with me."

"Fair enough; what would you like to know, Holden?" Ethan asked. He was terrified of the next question, but unlike his sisters or mother, this Cimoc tempered his words. Each word was chosen with meticulous care as if he did not want to walk too fast and have the words spill out of his bucket.

Holden asked him, "I heard the reason you gave to Janie for buying her the dress. Is that true or did you buy it because you were afraid she would go to dinner in a tee shirt that read: Deez are ma' titties?"

Ethan could not hold his laughter. "Truthfully man, a bit of both. I was in the store, the dress was there, it was pretty, and then I started to imagine the worst. I cannot even make my mind work like hers to fathom what the next shirt she would wear would say!"

There was still no smile on Holden's face. "You have no idea," he told Ethan.

His body language, relaxed now, softened the space between them. His countenance wasn't so gruff nor was he in a defensive stance. "My bike was down and I had to get to a job interview. Janie took me," he said.

The expression on his face had Ethan ready to laugh before the words fell from his lips. "She wore a fuchsia tee shirt that read: *Deez R Ma' Lady Nutz*! The back was worse than the front and the front had arrows pointed at the tips."

Ethan was choking back the laughter, "What did the back say?"

Holden's mouth twisted as he spoke, "The back read: *Mine are bigger than yours!*"

That did it for Ethan; he laughed so hard his stomach hurt. What made it even funnier was the look on Holden's face when he delivered the next few gems. "The thing that pisses me off more than anything was that she was right. I know I got the job because of her and that damned shirt. Even after I was hired, dudes I didn't even know were asking me to meet my sister!"

The laughter stopped when Meg did a wolf whistle as Janie walked down the steps. Ethan and Holden both stood still watching her descend the narrow stairwell. Holden was filled with emotion because this part of being a woman had never happened for Janie. There were no prom dates or romantic dinners out. She worked. She maintained the gaps in the financial hole in the family. She never got to be a girl or get dressed up for fancy dates. There were no nice men in her life.

The way she moved in the fabric said more than her words ever could. In the dress, it was evident that Janie felt pretty.

Holden offered Ethan a handshake that was readily

accepted. "You saw something that she needed more than any of us could have known," Holden said.

Ethan's stare was on Janie as he responded to Holden, "I think I needed this more than both us could have known as well."

Legs which felt like lead carried Ethan to meet her at the base of the stairs. "You look amazing."

"Thank you, Ethan. It is a lovely dress and the shoes are the perfect size," she told him.

He extended his arm, saying, "We don't want to overshoot our reservation time."

"Reservations? You mean we are not going to the all you can eat buffet?" She asked with a smile.

"It may be our last good meal for a while, partner," he said. "Let's make the best of it."

Ethan told Holden and Meg, "I won't keep her out too late."

They watched their big sister walk away. Neither of them had ever seen her like this. Meg commented first, "Was she wearing makeup, Holden?"

"And lip color..."

"Did I see polish on her toenails?"

"Looks like she shaved those hairy monkey legs, too," Holden said.

The bookstore was quiet. "Do you think Mom and Dad would approve of him as their son-in-law?"

Holden did not miss a beat, "Who cares? Janie was happier tonight than I have ever seen her in my life. To me, that is all that matters."

Meg stared out the window as Ethan opened the car door for her sister. "Holden, do you think he is a good guy...I mean, he is not going to be some user that is going to take her money and put us out of business?"

Each word was carefully chosen when he spoke, "I do believe that man is all about business. If it works for the business that is what he is going to handle first. Emotions don't seem to be the fuel which drives him. I stood toe to toe intentionally challenging him. That man is results oriented. He did exactly what was needed to yield him the optimal results."

"So he is trying to seduce her..." Meg asked.

"No, Meg. I think she has already seduced him. She has him displaying emotions he may not have realized he owned," Holden said.

Emotions were riding high for Jimmy Earl as he watched the love of his life in fancy new clothes climb into the fancy car with the fancy black man. *This will never do. That bastard is taking my girl out on a date.*

Jimmy Earl knew he had to start making some plans before it was too late. In a little while Janie would be in love and sharing her body with *that* man. Once that happened, he knew he would never have a chance with her.

Chapter 12. The Rising Action...

Dinner was a welcome break from what Ethan was normally accustomed to dealing with over a meal—Kate pressuring him for marriage. Ethan had not really dated as much as he would have liked. He had a few past girlfriends and outside of Kate, all of the relationships had ended amicably. The ladies understood that the bookstore was his vision, but Bartleby's was also his life.

When his grandmother passed, she left both him and Tallulah a nice chunk of change for college. He used half of it for his undergraduate work. A portion he used to buy inventory and to pay the first year's rent on the store. It was a very hard year. So hard, in fact, he looked forward to those Sunday dinners with his parents to make sure he had one good meal during the week. The rest of the time, his diet consisted of cheap noodles mixed with cans of vegetable soup. The irony was he ate better in college than he did as a small business owner.

In his heart, he knew that merging these two businesses was probably going to put him back in that same spot. If the apartments above the Roxy were useable, he may have to sell his place and live there as well to save money. All of these things he wanted to discuss with Janie, but her head was in the clouds. She looked so lovely and the last thing he wanted to do was ruin this night out for her with discussions of business.

"You look so beautiful, Janie," he told her.

"Thank you for this...the dress, dinner...you know I don't date. That store is my life and every penny I have is put into making it work," she said.

"Same here," he smiled at her.

The restaurant he chose was a four star steak house with tablecloths, cloth napkins, and a piano player. He truly enjoyed the live jazz singer but had stopped coming there to dine because Kate complained that the singer was off-key. The one thing he always wanted to do was dance while the jazz diva sang and tonight, he hoped to get that chance.

"Janie, will you do me the honor of this dance?" he asked before rising from the table. In case she said no, he didn't want to look like a fool.

"I can't dance, Ethan, and I don't know how," she said.

He rose from the table and extended his hand. "Lean on me and I will guide you."

Her blue eyes looked up from her plate and she asked, "In all things...?"

"In all things, Janie Cimoc," he told her.

In his arms, she melted like a pat of butter on hot corn. His right hand pressed gently into her back, guiding her movements as his left hand held hers. Their bodies swayed to the music as the jazz singer belted out lyrics, slightly off-key and too pitchy in some spots, but not once did Janie complain. One hand rested on his chest while the other was placed in his as her heart raced.

He understood this evening was something special to her and he did not want to disappoint. Ethan kept the conversation light as they shared information as a means of getting to know each other. He watched her portion out her steak, eating half of the meat and veggies and boxing up the other half to take home. *Frugal or broke?* The financial portions of the merger would require close scrutiny going forward; this he knew. He also knew something else; he wanted to kiss her.

Badly.

After dinner, they left the restaurant, walking past a homeless man who asked for some change. Janie slowed her step, "I don't have any money, but I can put something in your belly to get you through the night."

The dirty old man grinned at her with missing teeth as she handed him her carryout box.

"God bless you," the old man said to Janie.

She in turn looked at Ethan, "He already has."

Ethan was uncertain if his shoes had gotten tighter or his chest, but he felt bigger and taller, as if he had grown six inches in that very instant cradling a new understanding that Janie was a gift to him. How it would all work out, he was uncertain, but he drove her home pondering the possibilities.

"Where am I taking you, Janie?"

"Back to the shop," she said.

"To pick up your car?"

"No, I live there," she told him.

"You live in your bookstore?"

She tapped at his hand, "No, silly head; I live above it. I am hoping to have a similar arrangement at the Roxy."

"By the time all of the repairs are done and everything is moved in, I may be living up there with you," he told her.

When they pulled into the shop parking lot, everything was dark around the store front. *Not safe*. Ethan didn't like it. "I will see you inside and make sure everything is okay."

He stood watch, his back facing hers as she unlocked the main door. Inside the shadowy store, he could barely see in front of his fingers. "This is unacceptable Janie; what if someone was lying in wait for you?"

"Oh, stop being paranoid," she spoke as she clicked on the stairwell lights. "You want to come up?"

Ethan looked around the store a bit more. Checking behind the counter, under the tables, just to make certain no one was hiding inside. "No, I am going to head home; we have a busy day tomorrow."

In the soft light of the dim stairwell, never had a woman looked so radiant. Ethan was drawn to her. *I'm going to kiss her.* His arm slipped around her waist as he gently pulled her in close. His breath caressed her neck as he leaned in to inhale the scent of strawberries and peaches that clung to the strands of her hair. "You smell good enough to eat," he whispered.

"You are moving pretty fast, Part'Nuh," she said as she leaned into the maleness of him craving his touch, wanting him to kiss her. If he did, in Janie's head, it would be the perfect ending to a perfect evening.

Ethan was never one to intentionally disappoint a lady. His thumb stroked across her chin, gently encouraging her to open her mouth as he lowered his head, allowing his tongue to dart in between her lips, sweet like, but noninvasive. Janie moaned as she rose to her tiptoes to give him a full on kiss. Her mouth, hungry like a baby bird, continuously opened, swallowing, craving more. Greedy hands stroked his back as her nails razed across the cotton fabric of his shirt, sliding down his sides while collecting the fabric in a crumpled bunch in her hands. Her breasts pressed against his chest, wanting to be closer to him, urging him to get closer to her. Janie's hands left his sides and moved to the front of his pants, feeling, searching, looking for the knowledge to size up the man, touching him until she made contact with her target.

He jumped back. "That is my cue to leave," he told her.

"You don't have to...I mean, that is a nice dangling participle," she grinned at him in the low light.

Nature was drawing Ethan to her, but this was not right for the start of their partnership nor the right time for such intimacies. Too much was at stake and it could ruin their business before it even started.

"Good night, Janie," he said.

"You sure you don't want to bring that dangler upstairs to adjust my syntax?" She was laughing.

"I am adding a period to end this night and heading home," he said. "Call me tomorrow so we can make arrangements on the taxes on the Roxy."

"Okay," she said. Her face implied something else needed to be said.

"What is it, Janie?"

"Nothing...it was just a really nice evening. I truly enjoyed myself," she said.

He moved closer to her, "The best part was kissing you goodnight."

"Yeah, you need to leave now with your smooth talk and silver tongue."

It was a carnal gaze that curled her toes in her brand new sandals. His brown eyes made her body a solemn promise. "You have no idea, Janie."

"Now you have me craving an infusion of your stalker virus," she said as she pushed him towards the door.

"Let's take this a step at a time, okay? That's all I ask," he told her.

There was more she wanted to say, but common sense stepped in and took over. "Janie is okay with that as well. Goodnight."

Olivia Gaines

It wasn't fair. Ethan Strom was supposed to be her husband. It had taken six months of careful planning to get into his life and a whole year of nurturing him and prepping him to be her mate. Now, she sat on the outskirts watching like an unwanted interloper spying on a life that he was building with some blonde floozy. Kate was possibly one of the unhappiest people on the planet, and it was all Janie's fault. Eighteen months of careful, meticulous planning, all *stolen* by *her*.

Kate had seen Ethan in her library one spring morning as he perused the new arrivals section. Through the aid of some common friends, she found out more about the man and his bookstore. The number of single, attractive black men in Venture was small, and a man like Ethan was even more of a catch. He was an old school kind of guy who did not have a string of women that he'd been with in the small town, unlike most of the others who approached her. Those guys had dated every loose pair of panties in the quaint little borough, but not Ethan Strom.

On a quiet Thursday afternoon, she wandered into Bartleby's for a cup of coffee. Unobtrusively from the back of the room, she observed him interacting with his patrons. Nubile flesh in shorts and low cut blouses paraded themselves in front of him and she watched his eyes as he spoke with each woman. His eyes never strayed to their breasts or to watch tight little asses walk away. Curiosity led her into the book club discussion as he set the room up for the ladies, encouraging a hearty discussion, but warning the ladies about bad language. His smile was warm and Kate made up her mind that he was going to belong to her.

A few well-placed phone calls later, she had scored an introduction. Once she met him officially in person, she manage to score a date. A date to a mediocre steakhouse with a crappy jazz singer who nearly made her ears bleed. The conversation was good, the food not so much, but the company was divine. Kate called the next week to take Ethan on a date and he willingly accepted. It only took four more dates for her to get him into bed. From there, it was a regular Saturday night thing, dinner out and conversation with the evening ending with some good loving. But he never allowed her to stay the night and he never stayed the night at her place. She always assumed that it was because he was the Pastor's son, but maybe she didn't know him as well as she thought she had. Something else that bothered her more than she cared to admit, in the course of a year, his mother had never hugged her as she had observed Hester do with Janie. Hester had kept her at arm's length, with careful word choices, but never had she been to the Pastor's home or broken bread at their table.

A year and a half of my life.

Eighteen months of loving a man and planning to share a life with him; *stolen*. A beautiful life taken from her by an air headed, stupid tee shirt wearing, blonde trollop!

Ethan is mine.

She can't have him.

I won't let her.

Chapter 13. Laying Out the Setting...

By all accounts, the Roxy was in good condition. The termites had not moved in to create a walking all you can eat feast, there was no water damage, and the wood floors were intact. The real test revolved around getting two different types of bookstores into the space. The first thought that came to Ethan was to put the comics on the second floor, but if it were his business, he would want to be in the middle of daily floor traffic. He also wanted to see Janie all day, every day.

Get a grip on yourself, man.

She was an amazing woman. Today, she was wearing a blue tee shirt that read: *You can touch mine, if I can kick yours*. Armed with the power statement of a tee, Janie walked into the Mayor's office and began a hard core negotiation.

"These taxes are too high for that building," she told him.

"I am giving you a good deal; you pay half now and do the rest in payments," he told her.

"Or we can let that building stand there as a blight and do nothing. The traffic we would have brought to that area as well as your sister's store will be gone," she said.

"And what about your businesses?" the mayor wanted to know. "I made you the offer to save your businesses."

Janie was not budging, "You made us an offer on two buildings you knew we wouldn't take and the third was to help save your family's business, Mr. Mayor. We will take the Roxy, but for three grand and not the $4500."

"And what if I say no?" Mayor Galley asked.

Turning the Page

For a woman who stood at five feet five inches, she stood tall in his presence, "Then I will finally get to go to college and Ethan will head to grad school."

The Mayor leaned his chunky body back in his chair, which squeaked in protest every time he moved. Thick, sausage-like fingers interlaced together, connecting two fat arms over a bloated paunch as beady green eyes stared her down. Janie still did not budge.

"You drive a hard bargain there, Janie Cimoc," Mayor Galley posed. He looked at Ethan, who said nothing. In truth, Ethan had been willing to pay the $4500; he loved the space and it was worth it to be rent free and own the building outright.

The Mayor looked at Ethan, "You feel the same way she does, son?"

"She is a tough business partner, and her offer is fair...all things considered," he said. *Does he expect me to want to pay more than I have to for the building?*

The chair squeaked as the mayor's rotund body swiveled back and forth in the seat. "Fine, but don't come back asking for any more favors."

Three thousand dollars later alongside a signature and the collection of a deed, and Ethan Strom and Janie Cimoc were the proud owners of the Roxy.

In the car, Ethan glanced over at her. "You could have told me you were planning to negotiate so I wouldn't have stood there like some cuckolded fool looking like I was letting my woman do the heavy lifting," he told her.

Janie ignored everything else he said and focused in on two words, "Your woman?"

He shook his head. "You know what I mean...in the figurative sense."

The disappointment on her face was shielded by her staring out the window. "All I had to spare was $1500, so I had to get him down to my manageable half of the deal."

Something else was bothering Ethan, but he would get to it later. "Janie, I will need my accountant to go over your books. You will also have access to mine."

She shrugged, "No need. I clear about $45k a year after I pay Meg, Jem, and operational costs. I have about five grand to put into renovations. I put aside $300 to move all of my inventory and another grand to fix one of the upstairs rooms for me an apartment."

She went into her purse and pulled out a check for the five thousand. "It's all I have, but I'm willing to work hard to get things ready. We'll have Holden on the weekend, but Jem and Meg will have to mind the store while we work on the new space."

Ethan spoke to her in a flat tone, "So, we have a ten thousand dollar budget?"

"We are going to have to make it work for ten to get everything set up and ready. I do not want you to invest any more than I can as we are partners. I know your store probably makes four times what mine yields in a year, but I sell comic books. My business will bring teens and kids into the store, something you don't currently have. I will pull my weight. You won't have to carry me," she told him.

"Fair enough," he told her.

Ethan's initial assessment remained the same. Janie was an amazing woman. He was about to find out just how amazing she actually was.

Turning the Page

One of the great things about living in a small town was the convenience of having everything so close. The Mayor's office, located in the center of town in City Hall, also housed the major utilities departments. One phone call from the Mayor and the electricity and water were turned on before Janie and Ethan even left the building. While inside of City Hall, a new business license was also purchased for The Roxy-Books, Comics, and More. The last stop was to the bank to deposit funds and open a joint account.

At the end of the two hours, Janie felt like she had gotten married. She even told him so, "This is an odd feeling. We have created this new life together like some kind of newlyweds starting the next chapter of our relationship."

The goosebumps on Ethan's arms agreed with her; his mouth chose to stay muted as they drove to their new building. Frank, a high school friend of Ethan's, who worked for Venture's Waterworks Department, was coming from around the side of the building.

"Hey, Ethan! Yous the new owner of this building?" Frank asked him, the New York accent still heavy.

"Yes, Janie and I signed all the paper work this morning," he told Frank with pride.

"Yous got a good deal here. My brother-in-law Bob and me did the pipes on this joint a year or so before they closed. All new PVC...so the pipes are good. I think Frank even put in new filter systems for the catering kitchen upstairs," Frank told them.

All Janie heard was kitchen. She grabbed the key to the door that dangled freely from Ethan's hand, ran over to the building, and opened the front door. "I'm so excited!" Janie exclaimed as she opened the door and stepped inside the darkened room. Her hand made contact with the light switch and flipped it up, and the Roxy was alive.

Frank was still outside with Ethan as he handed him his card. "If yous guys need some repairs and construction done, we have the team of guys to come in and get it done right and on budget."

"I appreciate that Frank; thank you," Ethan told him. His mind was on Janie in that building.

He walked inside and gazed up at the ornate ceilings. The balconies were beautiful as well as the sturdy Corinthian columns which upheld the second floor decking. Janie's hand slipped into his as emotions flooded her.

"Ethan, this is ours," she whispered.

Before he could respond he heard a loud gust of air being exhaled by someone very pissed off. They both turned to see Kate standing behind them, and she was without a doubt very furious. Ethan wasn't far behind her feelings.

The second drawback to living in a small town was that everyone knew everyone's business; whether it concerned them or not. Nosiness was transcended in small towns to interference that was disguised as caring for the welfare of your fellow man. Ethan had no doubt that someone, who considered themselves to be Kate's friend, called to let her know that he had been in City Hall with Janie.

"This is bullshit! I am calling bullshit on the two of you! Did you pick up a marriage license while you were at City Hall as well?" Kate wanted to know.

She looked like a crazy person standing in the doorway. Her eyes were bugged, her hair was askew, and she was frothy about the mouth.

"Kate, what are you doing here?"

"I'm calling bullshit; that is what I am doing here. You can't expect me to seriously believe you met Goldilocks last week and now you have a shared bank account, bought a building, and started a new business all in less than seven days? I am not so dumb to believe you when you say you just met! It takes you two weeks to decide how many copies of a best seller you want to order…and this? All of this in less than a week? It's bullshit!"

Janie stepped forward, "No what is bullshit is you being some sort of crazed stalker!"

Her words incensed Kate even more. Kate's eyes were red as she charged towards Janie only to be caught in Ethan's arms. His voice was loud and firm when he looked at Janie, "Stay out of this, Janie. This is between me and Kate. You get started taking a preliminary walk through on this floor, open those drapes, and let some light in here." There it was again; his authoritative voice.

He looked at her once more and Janie had not moved. "Now Janie!" This time there was power behind his words followed by a firm stance that demanded obedience.

Ethan didn't know what to make of the expression on his partner's face as she walked away slowly. That, he would deal with later; right now his arms were full of a wild cat that he had to calm down.

"Kate, there are some big developments about to happen in Venture. In order for our businesses to survive what is coming, we had to combine forces. We purchased this building for the cost of the back taxes, but this is a logical step for what was next for both our stores. We get the expansion and also get the benefit of an equal partner to free up some of time so we can actually have a life," he told Kate.

She was still in his arms, leaning against his chest. "Ethan, I would have helped you build this. I would have helped you grow your business."

He held her close and planted a kiss on her forehead. "I know you would have, but my bookstore isn't your dream. Asking you to do that would not have been fair to you."

"Do you love her Ethan?"

"Who... Janie?" he asked.

"Yes...her. Are you in love with her?" Kate asked again.

"No, I am not," he answered truthfully.

Kate's next question hit him like a slug to his chest. "Did you ever love me, Ethan?"

He cradled her body in his arms, stroking her hair, or least trying to push it down against his chest as it stuck up and out in all directions. "I will always have love for you Kate."

"You were never in love with me were you?" She asked.

Again he was candid, "No, Kate, I was not."

Janie watched from the shadows as he comforted his ex with kind words. Embarrassingly enough, she had eavesdropped on how tender he was with her as he let her down and showed her out the door. She had not moved when he closed the front door and called her name. It was difficult for her to reconcile what she was feeling so she gave into everything that was effervescing to the surface. She didn't care if it was appropriate or not, she wanted him. Janie craved the touch of Ethan in the worst kind of way and she was going to have him even if it meant giving herself in lust on the dirty, dusty floor.

Janie's skin was rosy as she walked to the center of the cavernous space to respond to Ethan's call before her surrender to him.

"Are you okay, Janie? Your skin is so flushed; do you need some water?" He asked.

Her breathing was uneven as her fingers touched the fabric of his shirt.

"No," she answered huskily. "What I need is you."

Chapter 14. Adding More Tension…

"Whaaaa?" Ethan said, his mouth slightly ajar. "Janie, we have a lot to get done today. It is already after one, and I am starving."

Instead of answering him, she moved even closer, limiting the distance between them as her breath came out in shallow pants. Hesitant fingers touched the material of his shirt, pressing into the cotton, feeling the sinew of his muscles underneath. There was no fat or flab on his body. He wasn't squishy like the nerds who liked to hang out in The Comic Book. Ethan didn't smell like pepperoni pizza, Doritos, and a diet of too much sugar.

He smelled like a man.

A grown ass man.

"Janie, let's do a preliminary walkthrough, grab something to eat, and then come back to really walk the space to determine where we want to place what," Ethan said. He really was noticing the peculiarity of her actions. "Seriously, are you okay? Your face is really flushed."

Her fingers were making a trail across his abdominals, toying with the tight weave of the cotton of his polo shirt. She looked at him with desire in her eyes, telling him, "…I mean, I have read about women who have been overcome with these types of feelings…seriously, I thought it was all in jest, until you went all alpha male on me…and my body…wow…I am so turnt up right now, Ethan."

Her arms went around his waist as she pressed her body closer to him, "You smell so good."

"Janie, what in the hell is wrong with you?" Ethan asked as he tried to pull away from her.

"I want you, Ethan. Take me! Take me right here on this dirty floor!" she told him as she reached up and grabbed hold of his head, pulling his face down into her breasts.

It was an odd reality as Ethan found himself pulled into her energy. "This is not funny, Janie; stop it. I am a man. There is no on and off switch. The laws of gravity are slightly altered when it comes to men. What goes up requires some form of friction to come down," he told her as he pulled his face from in between her breasts with his eyebrows arched, hoping she would understand his analogy on male anatomy.

Janie's grip on his head increased as she sidled her body closer to his, and her right leg, slightly bent at the knee, slid up his left one while her tongue trailed down his neck.

"Damn!" he said as his hands came under her hips to take two handfuls of her bottom. His head lifted slightly for his mouth to make contact with hers and his tongue slipped between her lips. Janie moaned loudly into his mouth as Ethan hefted her off the floor into his arms. Her legs wrapped around his waist as he carried her to the nearest solid object he could find - a dusty table.

Ethan wanted to stop but she wouldn't allow him.

"Touch me, Ethan," she begged him.

His mouth moved to her neck, kissing her as his hands moved her skirt above her thighs. In Janie's world, she had never felt this way about a man. Since the age of 16 working in the comic book store, the only men she ever came in contact with were guys excited about the release of a limited edition poster or graphic novel. Those men were collectors of cards, players of games, and unkempt Peter Pans. Ethan was very virile and classy and reeked of something underneath the nice guy façade, which reverberated in her reproductive channels as him being a pack leader. Her body was screaming to mate with him. She followed the urge.

Ethan's fingers slipped under her skirt to make contact with the damp cotton that covered what his body craved; a place to create some friction. Pressure was applied with his index and middle finger to the center of the flower, spreading open the petals.

"Oh! My! Goooooodness!" Janie cried as she threw her head back as her knees came up to her chest, giving him more access.

His mouth found hers once more as their tongues dueled and his fingers made small circles in the cotton fabric that served as a barrier between him and the receptacle of resistance his body needed for relief. He would have none. Three more rubs with his fingers and Janie convulsed, twitched, and drooled out of the corner of her mouth.

"Janie?" he asked in disbelief. *Did she...?*

She was breathing hard, gnawing on her bottom lip with her eyes closed. Her nectar had saturated the pink cotton panties and Ethan looked at his wet hand.

Janie's eye lids were heavy. "I'm sorry; I couldn't wait. I will help you though. What do you need, my hands, my mouth..." she asked as she reached for his belt buckle.

It wasn't right. This was neither the time nor the place for him to be with her and he would not have her debase herself in a filthy building on her knees to pleasure him.

"I will be okay; besides, I was not prepared for anything more, but I would like one thing" he said to her. His lips pressed against her cheek then found her mouth again, kissing her softly.

She watched him coyly, wanting to give him anything he needed. "What would that be?"

He licked his lips, "...a taste..."

His eyes were smoky as he watched her face. Her knees, which had been closed after achieving her ecstasy, opened for him. The wetness of her underpants held the aroma of her ambrosia. Blue eyes met his brown ones as she watched his hand slip in between her thighs, gently pulling aside the cotton as he inserted his finger like he would into a bowl of batter. He scooped up a finger full of the nectar, bringing his hand up to his face, inhaling her scent like a bloodhound on the hunt. His tongue snaked out and curled around his finger as he loudly sucked at the liquid which covered his digit.

"Well, hell..." Janie said as she reached for her panties.

He stopped her, laughing out loud. "I'm hungry. Let's get some lunch," he told her.

"You can drink your fill right here- Janie would like that a lot," she said to him with a smile as she pulled her skirt up higher.

"Another time, Janie," he said as he adjusted himself in his pants. He hoped his discomfort would end soon. He had no desire to walk across the street and scare the crap out of Bitsy. He could see it now: *Yes Bitsy, I would like a BLT to accompany my raging hard-on.*

His fingers massaged his eyes. Between Kate, Janie, and the new business, he didn't know if he was going to be able to endure until the grand opening. He watched his business partner, her step full of spring, as she made her way across the street. She was as carefree as if she had not just half seduced him or was walking around with orgasm-soaked panties.

Olivia Gaines

He exhaled and looked upwards toward the afternoon sun. "I am not going to survive this..."

Chapter 15. Evolving the Characters...

The next two months were the longest of Ethan's life. The harder he tried to avoid being alone with Janie, the more he craved the feel of her in his arms. The taste of her called to him when he lay quietly in his bed at night. The strawberry and peach smell of her hair clung to the hairs in his nostrils, bringing the scent of her home with him. The bright side of the whole affair was that by the time he made it home at night, he was too exhausted to think of anything more than sleep.

The Roxy was a dirty place with so much potential that he was grateful for the blessings, and there were many. Janie was very blessed that school was out for the summer, which freed up Jem to help Meg manage Janie's store. Henry and Hester were also a major help to Ethan as they rotated days in the shop to work alongside Marta. This gave Ethan and Janie nearly 12 hours a day to work on the Roxy.

Twelve hours a day to smell her hair.

Twelve damned hours a day to watch the sweat bead between her breasts.

Twelve, long, thirsty hours of seeing her in those shorts; twelve hours of looking at those thighs, imagining the feel of them again around his hips. Twelve hours to feel like a horny pig for looking at her and watching her when she was not looking.

He was staring at a spot on the floor, one hand on the rented buffer and the other hand holding the wax. He had rented the buffer to take out the imperfections in the wood floors, but in the interim, the work was showing more imperfections in his character. After smoothing out the rough spots on the floors and stripping the old wax away, he was ready to put down a new layer of polish.

I know something else I want to wax.

He had not moved from his spot in almost eight minutes when Holden walked up behind him. It was another blessing that on Saturdays Janie's brother stopped by to lend a hand. Holden was great at repairing almost anything that was broken or dangling and at constructing shelves. It also helped that he was a certified electrician. Ethan gladly paid him whatever meager amount he requested to aid them with repairs.

"So, how bad do you have it?" Holden asked him.

"How bad do I have what?"

Holden, who rarely smiled, gave a half smirk, "How bad do you have it for my sister?"

During the past month and a half, he had been avoiding her, minimizing the time they spent in close confinement with each other. Their conversations centered on business choices and decisions, nothing personal.

"Holden, I don't know what you are talking about."

"Really? And staring at a spot in the floor for nearly ten minutes is normal for you, especially considering the raging piece of wood that is keeping you company."

Ethan looked down at the front of his pants and exclaimed, "Danggone it!" He tried to turn his back.

"No need to try to hide it; Janie already saw it. She was grinning like an idiot, which is what made me wonder what she was looking at," Holden told him.

Ethan untucked his shirt. "It is not like that, man. I have not been unseemly with your sister," he vowed.

Holden's facial expression did not change, "I have no

doubt about that, Ethan. You also have been going out of your way to avoid her and she's been going out of her way to make sure you can't."

"Whaaaaa?" Ethan asked.

Holden was actually laughing when he told him, "Janie never wears shorts, or halter tops for that matter. Outside of those stupid tee shirts, which she also has stopped wearing, she is usually covered up."

Ethan was shaking his head. "Man, I'm being honest with you. I'm trying my damndest. I want to keep everything professional between us. Getting involved physically or romantically could mean the death of our business."

"You don't seem to get it, Ethan. You may not have a choice. She has chosen you, and she has every intention of making you her own," Holden told him.

Holden patted him on the back, "The question is Ethan have you determined your terms for surrender?"

"You say it as if I have no say in the matter, Holden. I have every choice and as a responsible adult, I will make a responsible decision," he told Holden adamantly.

Holden wasn't buying it. "Sure. Let me know if that works for you. You are barely getting through waxing a floor, unless that kind of thing turns you on…"

"To be honest, you have no idea who or what I was thinking about; you can't automatically assume it was your sister," he told Holden, hoping to get the dude off his back and away from such an uncomfortable subject.

"Ethan, if Janie were black, would you have such a crisis in conscience?"

It was a question he didn't know how to answer. "It is not question of skin color. It just isn't right. I am going to have to work with her every day or buy her out if we do something stupid that doesn't work out. I have to eat. I have to live. I have a mortgage, a car note, and that damned Sallie Mae. I can't afford to risk all of that based on what…desire?" I can't and I won't."

Holden understood. "Just don't break her heart."

"I'm trying to be the good guy here," Ethan said, but the rest of his words were cut off.

The doorbell jangled and everyone looked up. Janie was working on the upper right side balcony and walked to the edge of the balustrade to see who had come inside The Roxy. Her eyes were drawn to the pretty, statuesque black woman. She reeked of class and money. Janie could tell the lady was someone important. The lady was also important to Ethan, who stopped his conversation with Holden to greet her at the door.

Janie was ashamed that she felt a tinge of jealously as Ethan embraced the lady. Maybe this was why he hadn't made any advances towards her; he'd left Kate for Ms. Classy Money Lady. *Her purse is worth more than everything in Janie's closet. Janie doesn't like the pretty classy lady.* She closed her eyes when she hugged Ethan. *Intimate. My Ethan is intimate with this woman.*

Holden was also watching her closely.

Ethan turned to introduce the lady. "Hey guys, come on over. I want to introduce you to my sister, Dr. Tallulah Strom."

Janie was dirty and covered in a layer of grime, but she didn't care as she threw her arms around Tallulah and her pretty linen suit. Ethan wanted to warn his sister ahead of time, but it was Janie. There was no preparing anyone for an encounter with Janie.

"What a pleasure to meet you," Janie said. She hugged Tallulah out of relief that she was not the new woman in Ethan's life as well as being genuinely happy to meet her. "Are you are doctor of letters or a doctor of medicine?"

Tallulah was so taken aback by the friendliness of her brother's new partner that she looked at Ethan, who only shrugged. She answered Janie's question, "I am a doctor of medicine. I'm a pediatrician," Tallulah answered.

"How hellacool is that?" Janie said with her nose scrunched up. "Come on, let me show you around our new store."

Ethan watched them walk off arm-in-arm, his sister surrendering to the enchantment that was Janie Cimoc. Janie's words were marinating in his brain. *Our new store.* Just like that, they were a couple. They were mated together as long as the store stood. However, he understood better than Holden or Janie ever could that the feelings in his pants didn't equate to feelings in his heart. He also understood that it was not time yet to negotiate surrender because he wasn't in the fight.

His heart he was not ready to surrender. He had been careful to keep it guarded, but Janie…she was wearing him down. *Maybe it is time…*

It was a quiet Saturday afternoon in the Comic Book. A few teens hung out in the back playing cards while other customers looked through trays of comics. Jimmy Earl had been in the store for nearly three hours and had not seen hide nor hair of his Janie. He knew he couldn't ask Meg or

Alice because they would give him some flip answer that would only make him madder than a caged up rattler. Instead he would ask Jem.

The teen was a lot friendlier than most of the family. Jimmy Earl slithered his way around the large table of Batman comics, coming up on the left side of the young man.

"Hey there, Jem. I haven't seen Janie around the store. Is everything okay with her?" Jimmy Earl asked.

Jem, thinking nothing of it, responded, "I dunno. I know Ethan has been keeping her tied up a lot lately."

One of his teen friends made an off-color remark that made Jimmy Earl's ears go all hot and get red at the tips. Jimmy Earl needed to know, "So Janie is dating that Ethan guy?"

"They're partners," Jem said offhandedly.

What he meant and what Jimmy Earl understood were two different things. "This will never do. Ain't no fancy pants dude gonna take my Janie away from me," Jimmy Earl mumbled under his breath.

I will give her one more chance to come back to me...

Chapter 16. Bonding the Characters...

It had to be the longest sermon Ethan had ever sat through. He wasn't sure if his dad was hyped up on sugar or too much coffee or had been visited by the Holy Spirit, but either way, Ethan was tired and wanted it over. His bed called to him for a midday nap; now that was something for which he was willing to negotiate a surrender.

"Ethan, are you coming to dinner with us this afternoon?" Hester wanted to know.

"No Mom, I am completely dead on my feet. I am headed to bed," he told her while he hugged his sister and shook his father's hand before pointing his car towards Delaney Street.

Inside of his overpriced tiny townhouse, he didn't even bother to undress; he loosened his tie, kicked off his shoes, and plopped down in his big daddy recliner. In his mind he wanted his bed, but his body only made it as far as the chair. His eyes closed in silent remembrance of a time when everything on him did not ache; within seconds, he was sleep.

An hour into an uncomfortable dream, which revolved around Janie and a pair of hot pink shorts that left little to the imagination, he awoke with a start. His phone was buzzing.

It stopped.

He closed his eyes.

It started buzzing again.

His first thought was to ignore the call and turn it off altogether, but he thought maybe something could be wrong with his parents. Reluctantly he answered it, not even bothering to look at the caller ID.

"Hello," he said groggily.

"Ethan, something's wrong with Johnny! He's not responding, and my mom is freaking out; I don't know what to do!"

At first Ethan had to remember who in the hell Johnny was. It was the youngest brother whom he had never met.

"Take him to the Emergency Room, Janie," Ethan told her.

"No! My parents don't like or trust doctors. His skin is clammy. His pupils are fixed and dilated. There is a temp....wait Mom...don't give him that!" She yelled at Alice.

"Janie, calm down. You have to maintain a level head," he told her.

"You maintain a level head. My brother is dying and these two stoned hippies will not let me take him out of the house!" She yelled.

In the background, he could hear her father telling at her to watch her tone. Janie hollered back, "You watch your tone! If you took him to the doctor like normal parents, he wouldn't be in this condition!"

Those were the two words which made Ethan act: *normal parents.* "Janie, text me the address."

Twenty minutes later, he pulled up in front of the double wide trailer with Tallulah in tow. The house, if it could be called that, looked like the backside of Woodstock where the people who never left resided. There were peace signs on the trailer. There were peace wind chimes, and wind mills in the shape of peace symbols were sitting beside garden gnomes holding peace signs.

Tallulah stepped one foot out the car asking, "What in the world?"

"Oh thank God, you are here! Tallulah, thank you. I will pay you whatever the rates are for coming out here; I don't care how long it takes to pay you for your time, I will do it...my Johnny...he is so sick..."

Inside the trailer was even stranger than the outside, starting with the orange, brown, and yellow shag carpet. Her father sat back with a giant joint smoking it as casually as possible while her Mom pulled fresh baked cookies from the oven.

Alice was smiling when they entered, "Janie told me we were having guests, so I baked some cookies."

"Good grief, Mom, your son is dying in the back room and you are baking frickin' cookies? Daddy," she yelled at her father. "Put that damned thing out. That is probably why he is sick; he is high as hell!"

Tallulah stopped at the door. "I cannot enter while he is smoking an illegal substance."

Janie moved so quickly that Ethan's eyes began to water. She doused the joint in water and yanked her father out of the chair and pushed him out the back door. "It's the best I can do, Doc," she told Tallulah.

"Show me where your brother is," Tallulah told Janie. Her eyes were on Alice, who seemed fixated upon the cookies and making coffee. Incredulously, Janie's mom was humming *White Rabbit*, and Tallulah garnered an immediate understanding of why Janie called.

The bedroom where Johnny lay was sticky and hot. "Let's get some fresh air in here. Get me a cool cloth, some ice, and water for him to drink," Tallulah said.

Janie rushed about collecting the needed items while

Ethan kept Alice out of the way. It did not take him long to understand that Janie's mother seemed to be disconnected from reality. Holden, Meg, and Jem came through the front door and spotted Ethan at the table. He nodded his head in the direction of Johnny's room, and all three took off down the hall.

Tallulah emerged from the room a few minutes later. "Janie will need to bring him into my office tomorrow for some additional testing, Mrs. Cimoc, but it looks like a case of the measles. We will need to update his vaccinations."

Holden spoke up, "What vaccinations? None of us were ever vaccinated?"

Everyone looked at Alice. "What?" she asked. "I was not going to allow the government to inject our children with toxins and tracking devices."

Janie stood up with her fists balled up at her sides. "I have to get out of here before I kill someone."

She stormed out of the door followed by Ethan and Tallulah.

"Go to her, Ethan," Tallulah told him.

"I will come back to her; first I need to get you home," he said.

Tallulah sat in the car, watching the trailer fade into the distance as her brother drove away. Janie, pacing in front of the shambled house, furious beyond reason. "That is an off family, Ethan," she told her brother.

"Yes, her parents were a part of that community of new agers and they never assimilated into regular society like all the others," he said.

"Oh, that commune of hippies from a few years back..." was all that Tallulah added. She was uncertain if Johnny was given the marijuana as a treatment for the measles or if the boy had a contact high from all the fumes inside to hot trailer. It was a toss-up whether or not Janie would bring the boy into her office tomorrow, but all of it was a waiting game. The measles had to run their course. The others, since they were not vaccinated, would probably also get infected. The other thing that troubled her was that this was the only case of measles in the whole county. Where could the kid have come into contact with a live virus? Tallulah had a lot of questions that were not going to get answered today. The only thing she could do was wait for her brother's direction before she did anything other than treat the boy.

Ethan arrived at the Comic Book to find Janie still sitting in her car. She was gripping the steering so tightly her knuckles were white. A light tap on the window pulled her out of her fugue. It took some coaxing to get her out of the car and into the building, but once they reached her living space, Ethan was at a loss for words for the third time in one night.

It wasn't an apartment, but a storage space with a small bathroom. The room held a small desk that also served as a dressing table. A clothes rack served as her closet. The twin-size bed had seen better days. An apartment-sized stove and fridge in a corner created a kitchen. There was a small sink and a hand-me-down table.

"It's not much but it's what I call home," she told him. She flopped on the bed and gathered her pillow close to her chest. "They aren't bad people, Ethan. They loved us unconditionally and did the best they knew how…they just didn't know much. As the others in the commune who traveled down here from Colorado with them moved away and took corporate jobs, my parents stayed true to their beliefs, even when it was to our detriment."

The tears had started to well in her eyes and she used the back of her hand to wipe her nose, "Holden and I have worked since we were teens and supported our family. Jem and Johnny are the last two in the house. We all work to make sure they have a normal childhood, but how can you protect a child from his own parents?"

Her tears were flowing while he pulled her into his arms. Janie pulled away from him, "Don't feel sorry for me, Ethan. I've worked hard to get what I have. It may not be much, but I have two more payments on this building and it is mine. Meg is starting college in the fall and Holden is a damn good electrician. He makes really good money. We even have a college fund for Johnny."

"What about you, Janie? You've taken care of everyone else; who takes care of you?"

"I take care of myself," she told him.

For some reason that didn't sit well with Ethan either. Janie was only 27. She started working in the Comic Book when she was only a teen so she could support her family. Ethan found himself wanting to take care of everything she needed.

"The moving truck is coming tomorrow, so you need a good night's rest. Tallulah will take care of Johnny and get him well. You have to make sure you are getting enough rest to stay healthy yourself," he told her.

Ethan planted a soft kiss on her forehead. "I will see you at the Roxy in the morning. I saw everything was packed downstairs and ready to go."

She only nodded.

"Come on downstairs and lock up," he told her.

Outside, Jimmy Earl watched Ethan leaving Janie's upstairs private space. The idea of what they could have been doing up there made Jimmy Earl start pulling at the stringy hair that hung from his head. *Janie is cheating on me with that fancy bastard! I will fix them both. They will not make a fool out of me!*

Chapter 17. The Game Changer...

Ethan couldn't believe he had overslept. He was plumb tired and weary down to his bones. His initial thoughts on the upstairs space in the Roxy was going to be an open loft type of living area, but he had an idea that he was certain she was going to love. He added a few extra dollars to the budget and worked after Janie left to make it a homey spacey. The end result was going to be great, especially after he had seen how Janie had been living. He knew starving artists in New York who lived better than she did in that hovel; some changes were coming. *What are you doing, Ethan?*

It was after ten when Janie arrived at the Roxy. The moving truck had picked up everything from her shop and delivered most of it; the moving men had set the tables and racks in the exact locations they had chosen. Janie's comics were located on the left side of the main auditorium. Many of the racks, along with items that were slow sellers, were placed under the balconies in the walkways. Since the areas were not well lit, Janie thought it would be more cost effective in the long run to string Christmas lights under the balconies as opposed to directional lights that would use more electricity. Ethan didn't think it was true, but it added a magical effect to the space and he liked the feel of the room.

The transformation of the space would be welcoming to customers. The front of the house had a brass covered bar that was used to sell wine and refreshments to the music hall customers. It was now going to be used to house his beautiful copper coffee maker. The movers were coming tomorrow to move his store to The Roxy and he was excited that they were almost ready to open.

The word also came in that the new big box bookstore was breaking ground as well. They had a few months lead time on the corporate machine to make The Roxy the best place to get books and more in the town of Venture. True, they could not stave off the glitz and newness of a big box store, so a homey folksy appeal was going to have to work. If there was anything Janie could provide, it was a homey folksy appeal.

"This looks really good," he told her while he aided in the placement of the last table. Many of her shelves did not make it to the store; they were too high for placement under the balconies. The game tables, with the exception of Middle Earth, were placed in the gutted balcony areas, with the four boxes becoming four separate play areas. The *Yu-Gi-O* area *and Game of Thrones* play tables were fixed. The other two would vary for game play as well as be used for chess or checkers. Thus far, the calmness of the store was going to be a great place for family and friends to connect.

Jimmy Earl peddled his way to the front door of the Comic Book. It was 7:30, just a half hour before closing. That would more than enough time for him and his Janie to work out some of the finer details of their relationship. Confusion overrode the amorous side of him as he saw the store was unlit, like it was closed. A sign on the door read: Join us July 4th Weekend for our Grand Reopening.

The sign gave an address for the new location on Candlestick Street. *That is way 'cross town. How are we going to continue our love for one another if she is way 'cross town?* Jimmy Early knew that if he was in better shape, he could ride his bike over to Candlestick and back and still make curfew at the halfway house before 10:00 each night. *It wasn't fair. What Janie is trying to do me ain't fair.* Jimmy Earl was hit with a dizziness akin to vertigo throwing him off balance. He didn't like the feeling.

He would show her how imbalanced felt.

The sense of calm was short-lived for Ethan. It was after midnight when Ethan's phone began to buzz. His hand was asleep as it groped in the darkness to find the disturbing noise that had interrupted his sexy dream of Janie in a hot red bikini running down the beach.

"Hello," he mumbled in the phone.

"Ethan, wake up. It's Holden," the voice said.

He sat straight up in the bed. ""What is wrong?"

Holden took too long to respond. Ethan was on his feet, half wearing a pair of sweat pants, his keys in his hand, and down the front stairs. He didn't know where he was going but he would start with the Comic Book. If she wasn't there, he would head to her parents. His heart was bumping against his rib cage as he heard the first siren roll past, then another, followed by two police cruisers. It didn't matter what Holden was saying to him on the phone; Ethan had hung up.

He drove as fast as he could to the Comic Book, arriving to see the flashing lights. It was the blaze that nearly stopped his heart. The car was barely in park when he jumped out and ran toward the flames screaming, "Janie? Janie?"

Holden grabbed him before he ran into the burning building. "She's safe, Ethan. She's over here."

"Janie...Janie, are you okay?"

"No! Someone set my building on fire with me in it, Ethan!" She told him after she ran into his outstretched arms. "I barely made it out alive."

Her face was smeared with dirt and soot. Her hair was singed and she shook like a leaf in his arms. "Who would do this, Ethan?"

Ethan didn't have an idea, but Holden was leaning towards that sniveling coward Jimmy Earl Leenes.

The tears overcame Janie. "Everything I own is in that building. Who would do this to me and leave me with nothing? I don't understand..."

She sobbed into his shirt, "I have nothing!"

Ethan lifted her into his arms and carried her to his car. "You have everything, Janie, and most of all you have me."

He nodded to Holden as he secured Janie in the car and drove toward Delaney Street. She would have to stay with him until the Roxy was ready for her to move in to the new space. In the interim, he would take care of her like she deserved.

The buckles that had been holding his heart in freeze mode gave way. Janie needed him. She needed his compassion and she needed his love. Both, he was resigned to give to her.

Chapter 18. Breaking Down the Conflict…

Janie was barefoot. The only thing she personally owned was what she was wearing on her back. Whoever torched her store also torched her beat-up old Volkswagen Bug. This attack on her was personal.

Ethan started the kettle before he filled up the tub with warm water. *Thank goodness I cleaned the bathroom this morning.* She watched him walking to the bathroom with the container of dishwashing liquid.

"What is with the dishwashing liquid?"

"Well, if it works on baby birds covered in slick from oil spills, it should work on removing that soot and singe from you," he told her. "Besides, it's the closest thing I have to bubble bath."

A lone tear rolled down her cheek. "Ethan, what am I going to do?" She implored of him.

"Take a bubble bath. That is all you can do tonight. Give me those dirty things you are wearing, and I will wash them. While you are soaking, I will get you a clean tee and some skivvies; I have an unopened pack. I can get you a safety pin."

Gently guiding her by the hand, he led her to the bathroom. There was a futon in the second bedroom that he made up for her with a spare pillow and blanket. He added a couple of drizzles of honey into a mug with a finger of whiskey and some hot water and lemon juice. The toddy would do well to settle her nerves so she could sleep.

"Ethan," she called to him.

He stood at the bathroom door. "Yes, Janie?"

"Will you come in and wash my back?"

"Hell no," he told her. "I have a toddy out here for you and the futon is made up in the guest room. Don't stay in there too long."

He loaded the dirty clothing she had left outside the door into the washer, set the machine to clean a small load in a cold water wash, and headed to his bed. He knew he wasn't going to get any sleep, but he was going to try. His moving day was tomorrow, and he needed as much rest as he could get. He already knew it wasn't going to happen and tonight would probably be one of the longest in his life.

He was right.

Janie didn't bother to go to the guest futon, but marched right through his bedroom door, pulled back the covers, and slid into bed with him. To make certain Ethan knew she was there, she grabbed his arm, pulled it over her, and plopped her handful of ass against his thighs.

"Janie, I made up the futon for you to sleep on tonight," he told her.

"Yes, but there is someone trying to kill me," she responded.

"So you thought it would be a good idea for them to get me, too?" he asked as he pushed her to the other side of the bed.

Janie scooted back underneath him. "We are in this together, Baby." She laughed as she snuggled close. The sound of their breathing filled the empty spots in the room. "Seriously Ethan, I am scared out of my mind. Someone set my building on fire...with me in it...and I think they knew I was inside. Why would anyone want to kill me?"

"I don't know Janie. Let's get some sleep and we'll tackle it tomorrow," he told her as his chin rested atop her head.

She stayed quiet for five minutes before she began to wiggle her hips against him. "Ethan..."

"No! Go to sleep," he said with a firm voice.

"But..." she mumbled into the fleshy part of his arm. "...you feel so good."

Ethan knew she was experiencing a delayed reaction to losing everything she owned, so he spoke softly into her ear, "You have experienced a major trauma and you're vulnerable. I would feel like I took advantage."

"I wouldn't feel that way," she whispered.

"I would. I have to live with my actions. If or when there is a time for us to go that route, it will happen on its own course," he told her.

"I'm really scared, Ethan..." She said it again, but this time it did not have the same meaning as it did when she said it out of fear for her life; this had a different connotation.

"Tell me your fears, Janie," he said softly.

She pulled away from him and settled her head into the pillow. She was facing him in the dimly lighted room, which only had a faint light from the kitchen striking the space they were sharing. "I am afraid that I will always love you more than you will love me."

His hand reached out to caress her chin, "I don't think that is possible; now get some sleep."

Even after declaring his love for her, it took everything in his will to turn his back to her and try to sleep. He closed his eyes and began to pray for understanding. If she called his name once more, he knew his strength would fail him, so understanding of the situation was what he needed to get through the night. His prayers must have been answered because Janie was asleep. More importantly,

Janie was safe.

Ethan sighed deeply as his father's words crept across his thoughts, "the only woman who should spend the night in your bed should be your wife." He had always held those words dear, and until this night, no woman had ever stayed the night with him, nor had he ever stayed the night with a woman.

Damn, Janie.

Surrender seemed a forgone conlusion in Ethan's mind. For some reason, he was okay with it.

The smell of sausages sizzling in a frying pan woke Janie. Sleepily rubbing her eyes, she made her way to the kitchen to find Hester standing over the stove. Hester poured pancake batter onto a griddle and picked up the kettle to pour hot water over a tea bag.

"Oh! You're up. Good morning, Janie," she told her as she set a small plate of sausages on the table.

"Good morning, Mrs. Strom," she said softly. *Where's Ethan?*

"Ethan told me what happened to you, and My Jesus, child, I am so sorry. After we have breakfast, I'm going to take you shopping. I guess at some point I will have to take you to the DMV to get a new driver's license and all that stuff as well."

Janie was eyeing the sausages. Her mouth began to water when Hester set the pancakes on the table. She was ravenous. "No, for some reason, I actually forgot my purse yesterday, so it is still at The Roxy. I got up last night to get my phone out of it to charge it up when I realized I didn't have it. That was when I smelled the smoke..." Janie shivered.

Hester gave her a warm hug. "Don't worry, you're in good hands. Let's get you fed, dressed, and ready to go shopping. I brought a sundress that I think you can wear and some sandals, so we will have you outfitted in no time at all."

Janie burst into tears. *Why can't I have this with my own mother?*

In a flash, Hester gathered Janie in her arms, rocking and smoothing down her hair, which would need to be cut and reshaped after the fire damage. "Janie, God sends us what we need exactly when we need it. Now come on before this gets cold."

Hester blessed the food and mid-way through her fourth pancake, Janie started to talk. It was something she had been wanting to tell someone all of her life and never had anyone to say it to...until now.

"My parents are not bad people; they are just clueless in the ways of the world. I was born on a cooperative commune in Colorado. My parents, once they married, followed an enigmatic man named Homer from the commune here to Georgia. It was their intent to start a new branch of the cooperative. It went well for a while, then Homer left my dad in charge when he moved on to Dahlonega to open another branch," she told Hester.

"My Dad is not a leader. Even on a good day, his best is to be a follower," she said as another tear ran down her cheek.

"We were damned near starving when I took the job at the Comic Book and honestly, I think Mr. Habersham gave me the job because he knew...but I worked hard, Mrs.

Strom. I earned my check. I even made a few bonuses, which kept fuel in the generators to keep our lights on. I began to understand how to survive in the world my parents despised," she said.

Janie went on to explain how she got Holden a job as an electrician's apprentice one summer. With their combined part time incomes, they were able to make repairs to the trailer, buy decent food, and ensure that everyone went to bed with a full belly. "Nothing scars a child like hunger, Mrs. Strom. I was not going to let Meg, Jem, and Johnny grow up like Holden and I did." She bit into a sausage as she wiped away another tear.

"No, Ma'am. Meg starts college this fall and Jem is heading into his junior year of high school. He's a talented artist and is going to be someone," she said.

"I am going to be someone as well. It may take me a bit a longer because I have to take care of my sister and brothers, but I will get there, Mrs. Strom. This is only a setback, but this ain't shit in comparison to what I have endured living with those two clueless hippies as parents. So don't feel sorry for Janie because Janie is a scrapper. Janie is going to be just fine!"

Her back was straight as she wiped her face. Pride sat on her shoulders when she faced Ethan's mother, wearing the drawers and tee shirt of Hester's son

"Janie," Hester spoke. "That day I met you in Bartleby's was one of the lowest days in my life. I had just lost my dearest friend and there was a hole in my heart so big and wide from missing her that I didn't know how I was going to get through the day, let alone my life without her."

She was grinning at Janie. "You saw a sadness in me and embraced me full on, surrounding me with love because you knew that was what I needed at that very moment."

Janie started to cry again as Hester spoke. "I am here not because I feel sorry for you, but to return the favor. I will surround you with as much love and support as you need."

Hester stood and opened her arms for Janie to run into. It was the kind of hug that made a person close their eyes in order to fully enjoy it. The kind of hug that made a child feel that everything was going to turn out just fine. Ethan was lucky to grow up with such a loving Mom.

Chapter 19. Getting to that Climax...

Ethan was so tired he could barely drive. He made it home a little after six with Janie's purse slung across his shoulder. It had been his intention to stop and pick up something to eat, but he didn't have a house phone and found out that Janie's phone was in her purse after he called her and followed the sound of the *Dance of the Sugar Plum Fairies* to her bag. He even called his mother, but found out that she had dropped Janie off hours ago with her brother.

He only hoped she would call. He found himself worrying about her as he inserted the key in the lock to let himself in. Inside, he walked into a surprise.

Candles were lit on the table. A bottle of wine was chilling and Janie was in the kitchen pulling garlic bread from the oven. She said nothing as she smiled at him. A glass of wine was poured and placed in his hand along with a fresh towel and wash cloth.

"Okay, I like this," he told her as he made his way to the bathroom to wash the day from him.

When he returned to the kitchen, a plate of roasted chicken with fingerling potatoes and mini carrots was made and set before him.. "This looks amazing, and so do you," he told her.

The long blond hair was gone and she sported a pixie cut. The orange sundress she wore brought out the peachiness in her skin and Ethan found he was having trouble concentrating on the meal.

Janie still had not said anything.

"You are uncharacteristically quiet," he said to her.

"I figured tonight I wouldn't make a fool out of myself by trying to get you to make love with me. You love me like a good friend. I am grateful for what you did for me last night, so I cooked you a meal to say thank you," she said.

Ethan had stopped chewing and sat watching her. *She has totally misread everything.*

"It is a lovely meal," was all he could think to say, versus what was actually on his mind.

"Holden will be by at 8:30 to pick me up, and I'll stay with him until I can get the space above The Roxy ready for me to live in," she told him.

This wasn't right.

He rose slowly from the table to retrieve his phone. He scrolled though his recent calls to locate Holden's number. Ethan pressed the button to dial Janie's brother. Holden answered on the third ring

"Hey, it's Ethan...I'm negotiating my terms for surrender," he told Holden.

"So I don't need to pick her up tonight?"

"You won't need to pick her up ever again. She is home," Ethan told him.

"Welcome to our crazy-ass family," Holden told him before hanging up.

Janie was only half listening. "What do you mean by surrender?"

"It has taken everything in me these last four months to keep my hands off you, and last night nearly broke me. I want you, Janie. I want you so badly that I am working myself to the bone so I will be able to go to bed and not be tormented with thoughts of you running through my head...keeping me up at night with longing," he told her.

Janie's cheeks became rosy. Her face was flushed like it

was the afternoon in The Roxy, where on the dusty table Ethan brought her pleasure with his fingertips. This brought back another memory; his finger in her batter. "The taste of you has been burned so deeply into my brain that every time you walk past me, I want to drop to my knees and drink my fill."

Janie was stammering, "Whaaaaa....are...ahhh...whaaa...are you saying, Ethan?"

"I'm through talking, Janie...I'm not saying anything else," he told her. He was out of the chair and on the floor in front of her. Strong hands turned the dining room chair, her body still in it, to face him. Ethan pushed the dress up her thighs, gripped her by the hips, and pulled each of her legs over his shoulder. The heat of his breath penetrated the soft cotton of her panties as he inhaled deeply and blew hot air into her flower.

"Damn," Janie said as she arched her back opening her legs to give him more access.

Ethan used two fingers to pull the fabric to the side as his tongue explored her femininity. Janie hips rose to meet the onslaught of his mouth, crying out his name as her hips moved against the pleasure he was bringing her. The sound of him slurping at her nearly drove Janie beyond the point of reason. She started to convulse, then twitch.

"Oh, no you don't. Not this time..." he told her as he rose to his feet, bringing her body with him. In one motion, he lifted her over his shoulder with her butt turned up in the air. He smacked it softly while telling her, "...You are not finishing without me."

He carried her to the bedroom and dumped her like a sack of potatoes onto the bed, "Clothes...off...now..." he told her as he pulled his white tee over his head. The drawstring on his lounge pants was pulled, allowing the fabric to pool at his feet. He stood at the side of the bed completely nude.

Janie had stopped fumbling with her dress. Hester had taken her to a Goodwill in the nicer part of town and picked out an entire wardrobe for less than $60.00. She leaned back on her elbows and stared at him. "Whoa...wow...hmmm...wow," she told him.

"No wonder Kate has been stalking you. You look...wow, look at that..." she pointed at his person. "...Whoa....I want it!"

She bounded to her knees and tried to grab him. He moved to the side. "Undress for me, Janie," he said to her again. This time his voice was unassailable.

She fumbled with the buttons down the front of the dress, trying to unfasten them. Giving up, she pulled the dress over her head. "I don't know exactly what to do, but you can show me...teach me how to please you, Ethan," she said.

Ethan froze where he stood, "What do you mean?"

Janie removed her bra and threw it at him. "I have never done this before...I mean... I've never done it before with a man."

"Whaaaaa..." Ethan said.

Janie was crawling across the bed, trying to get out of her underwear in the most undignified manner. "I never met a man who turned me on, unlike now. I am so hot for you I am about to combust."

Ethan still had not moved. "Janie, please explain," he said as he took a seat on the side of the bed.

"Nothing to explain, Baby," she told him as she reached for him. "Because I never met a dude who turned me on, I thought maybe I was gay. So I dated this lesbian." She leaned forward and kissed his neck as she massaged him in her hand. "Janie didn't like that shit."

Her breasts were pressed against his back. "Janie likes this a whole lot," she told him as her hand enclosed around him. She maneuvered him back and forth like it was a gear shift. "Janie likes this a whole lot. I want it! Give it to me, Ethan!"

"I am the first man to be with you intimately," he said softly. He removed her hands from around his person as he leaned forward to pick up his tee shirt. He waved the shirt in the air over his head.

"What are you doing, Ethan? I am ready to make love with you," Janie said, completely befuddled by his actions.

"I, my dear Janie, am waving the white flag of surrender," he told her as he lay back on the bed.

"Okay fine, but can you surrender after you make love with me? Seriously Ethan, I am naked, showing you 'ma titties...I'm ready. Come pluck ma' delicate flower," she told him.

"I'm going to do more than pluck it," he told her as he reached for her. "So...Janie, do you want a church wedding or something outside..."

He pulled her close as his mouth found hers.

"Later, Ethan...we will discuss that stuff much later," she said as her nails sunk into his back. His fingers worked slowly as his lips learned every inch of her body. She screamed his name as he connected their bodies, moving in unison in the soft light of the room as he created enough friction to bring them pleasure. Janie held him tightly as his pace increased, delving deeper into her petals, stroking the stamen with each downward stroke of his body.

Ethan could not hold back any longer. He wet his thumb before using it to rub the nub of flesh. It drove Janie wild as she bucked against him, yelling at the top of her lungs, "Janie likes it! Janie likes it!"

"Ethan likes it too Janie," he growled as he increased his pace, slamming into her over and over until he was drained. They collapsed in a sweaty heap. Ethan knew he had surrendered himself to her love and he would never be the same again. Neither would his Janie.

"Janie, can we work on that whole third person thing? It's kind of distracting," he said.

"Shit, that was so good, I wasn't sure if it was real or what! Both me and my subconscious were enjoying that immensely," she laughed.

"You were magnificent," he told her.

"And you... were everything I knew you would be," she told him as she snuggled closer and drifted off to sleep.

Tomorrow there was so much to do that tonight required rest. He held Janie close in his arms, inhaling the sweet strawberry and peach scent of her hair. The pixie cut was something he would have to get used to, but waking up with her in his bed and his arms was something he could easily get become accustomed. Life was going to be grand.

Chapter 20. The Falling Action…

Something wasn't sitting well with Holden. The whole morning felt off-kilter. Deciding to get to work late, he called his boss to let him know that he would be along as fast as he could. His first stop was the Comic Book, where he found Jimmy Earl sitting in the parking lot crying.

"Jimmy Earl! Stop all that carrying on and get yourself together," Holden yelled at him. It startled the weird little man, who pointed at the building.

"What happened to our store? Is my Janie okay? Who did this?" Jimmy Earl said through ugly tears.

In truth, Holden had assumed it to be Jimmy Earl who set the fire, but the next five minutes made him realize his sister's life was in serious danger.

"I tried to ride my bike over to the new store, but it was too far, and 'ma legs and 'ma lungs gave out. It was way past curfew when I got home. I was in a lot of trouble. I have been on lockdown for three days," Jimmy Earl confessed.

If not him…then who?

"Janie is fine, Jimmy Earl," Holden told him, but a niggling feeling crept up the back of his neck. *No she isn't.*

"Go home, Jimmy Earl," Holden said as he broke into a run to get to his truck. He drove as fast as the speed limit allowed to get him across town to The Roxy. He arrived, sweaty and out of breath.

Janie was nowhere to be seen and he faced Ethan panting. "Janie… where's Janie?"

"She's in the back, Holden. What is wrong?" Ethan asked.

"The fire..." Holden started to say but the doorbell jangled. It was Kate; her face was full of concern and emotion. Her hair was still askew.

"Ethan, you must be devastated. I came as soon as I heard. I know you are heartbroken losing Janie in that fire," she said as she threw her arms around him.

Janie came out of the back, "What are you talking about, Kate?"

The look on Kate's face said it all. She had not expected to find Janie in the store, let alone alive. "Three times I have tried to get rid of you! You filthy piece of trailer trash! Ethan is mine! He is mine!"

Kate took off at a sprint after Janie, who took off at a dash around the table, trying to get out the front door. Holden ran after Kate and slipped, falling over a stack of books and landing on his backside. Ethan had to think fast to give Janie a chance to get some help; he called out to Kate.

"Kate, Baby, come over here. Janie is not important to us. I was a fool, Kate. I should have never attempted to do any of this without you. I knew better than try to build this without your help," he told her.

She stood in the middle of the floor, eyes wide, chest heaving, with a crazed look about her eyes, "You are just saying that so I don't kill your pretty little blond sex toy!"

"Kate, Sweetheart, if you are in prison, then we can't be together. Killing her would get in the way of our dream," Ethan told her. His eyes were on Holden, who had managed to get back to his feet. Janie had not stopped when she ran to the front door, but she also ran out of it and across the street to ask Bitsy to call the police. It may have only been a few minutes, but to Ethan it felt like a lifetime.

Turning the Page

The crazy woman was yammering on about the attempts she made to get rid of Janie. "I thought if I convinced that crazy hillbilly Jimmy Earl that she loved him, that he would do something to separate you two, but no…"

Holden listened in disbelief.

"I also thought that infecting her little brother with the measles when he came into the library would show you how crazy her family was…how they lived like animals…no vaccinations…but you went and got your sister to help her!"

She charged at Ethan with a knife that she pulled from her purse, "If I can't have you, Ethan, neither will that bitch!"

A police officer with a stun gun came through the door and zapped Kate with enough volts to loosen her bladder. The knife hit the floor with a clank of metal against the wood, followed by a slobbering convulsing Kate.

As the officer escorted Kate out, Janie slowly walked back in the doors, her mouth wide as she tried to process the reality of it all. She looked at Ethan, saying, "That crazy bitch was trying to kill Janie!"

"You are safe now, Honey," Ethan told her as he pulled her into his embrace. "You are safe."

"I hope so; we have our grand opening next week. You don't have any more stalkers out there do you?" she asked Ethan.

Holden piped up, "I think I pulled my muscle in my butt cheek. I'm thinkin' I may be able to get that pretty sister of yours to make a house call." He rubbed his handful of bum. "Hey guys, speaking of which, I ran into Jimmy Earl. He says this is too far for him to ride his bike and get back to his halfway house before curfew."

Ethan didn't understand how that concerned him or how his butt cheek connected to Tallulah, but Janie did. "Holden, as soon as I get a vehicle, I will make a trip to the group home and leave some bus passes and show them how to use the bus system to get here," Janie said. She was still shaking a bit. "The group home makes a small monthly donation for us allowing the harmless ones to come and hang out once a week."

"Oh," Ethan said. He looked down at her with eyes full of love. "I would have never allowed Kate to hurt you."

"I know, but it was still scary. I know how she feels, though. I'm head over heels in love with you, but I don't think I would try and kill someone to be with you," she told him.

"That's good to know," he said as he looked over at Holden. "I guess now is as good of time as any," Ethan said as he took to one knee. "Janie Moonray Cimoc, will you marry me?"

Hester and Henry walked into The Roxy at that exact moment. Henry, who had not spent any time with Janie, asked loudly, "Moonray! What are your parents, hippies?"

Both she and Holden turned around and answered together, "Yes, they are. Long story. Don't ask."

Janie looked back at Ethan. "Janie sure would love to be Mrs. Ethan Strom, for better or worse, poorer or crazy, we are all in."

"That too…is good to know," he said as he rose and took her in his arms for a tender kiss.

Chapter 21. The Denouement…

No one could have predicted how turning up for a meeting on an offer for a business merger could have turned the page for all of those around the couple as well. The Roxy opened with a ribbon cutting ceremony and a parade with the local high school. No one understood why the owners waited until the end of the month of July to open, but Ethan and Janie needed a week for a honeymoon.

The wedding was a small ceremony in the Greater Mount Zion Baptist Church among friends and family. Many made comments out loud that Ethan was marrying a white girl, while others commented on a white girl getting married to Ethan. It didn't matter to either owners of The Roxy; they were happy. The honeymoon was small, with a trip to Orlando because Janie wanted to enjoy Universal Studios and visit Sea World. Initially, the honeymoon was not on the table until the insurance company came through with the settlement on the Comic Book. The saving grace was no inventory had been in the building.

It also helped to have a police report that proved a crazy woman had burned down the building. No clarification was ever achieved on how Kate got her hands on a live measles virus or how she even knew that Johnny had not been immunized. Janie chalked it up to some of Kate's *friends* attempting to do her a solid so she could 'keep her man.'

Ethan was thoroughly enjoying being a kept man. Janie was learning to refer to herself in first person and dealing head on with issues that troubled her, mainly her father. With the assistance of Tallulah, she managed to get her father into a rehab program only to find out he actually had testicular cancer. Alice, after attending the church service, fell in love with the Greater Mount Zion Baptist Church and became a member. Alice, who had never driven in her life asked Meg to chaffeur her to church each Sunday.

In less than three months, the bookstore was thriving. It was doing so well that the big box store decided there was not a big enough market to open a new store in Venture, Georgia. The groundbreaking was as far as the company went towards the new store.

"Come on in, come on in," Hester told the customers. It was Thriller Thursday and the book club was headed up to the balcony to meet. On the stage, Gandalf the Gray read to the Hobbits while the overhead projector layered the map onto the stage of the Shire. Ethan came up with the idea that instead of having a table top display, they would use the stage and project Tolkien's map of Middle Earth onto the stage floor. As the action moved between locations, so did the map. This week, they were at the base of the Lonely Mountain.

The apartments on the second floor were converted to living space for the Stroms, with two bedrooms, a soundproof writing lab for Ethan, and a new studio for Janie's Tee's, which were sold exclusively in The Roxy and via Janie's new website. Between the website orders and her new college classes, Mrs. Janie Strom was a busy lady. She worked in the bookstore on the weekends and some evenings, but comics were no longer her life.

Jem, Meg, and Marta still manned the counters, with Henry manning the coffee maker on Thursdays. Alice in the upstairs kitchen, bringing down trays of freshly baked goodies. His mother was engaged in a stimulating conversation with Dottie Meribodie about the new book to be read next month and the importance of character development.

"I have cookies!" Alice said as she set the tray on the table by the counter. She pulled back the cover and like ants, children began to materialize from everywhere. Parents did drive-bys, unloading mini-vans kids, along with the normal weekly loads from station wagons, BMWs, Fords, Mercedes, and everything else, including bicycles ridden by kids that came through the door at ten minutes of six. That same kid dressed like Sméagol slid in the door sideways, dragging his left foot this time, climbing the stairs to the stage to follow Gandalf. He reached up to grab a cookie from the passing tray that Alice carried, called it 'my precious," and took his place on a stool on the stage.

It was also editing night for Ethan. He was in his writing lab making changes to his latest novel. A regional publisher had picked up the manuscript and gave him a three book deal. Angus McCraffey fell in love with Ethan's words and hilarious characters. His first novel was due in books stores by Valentine's Day.

A newcomer to Venture walked into The Roxy, amazed at what he was seeing. Two worlds combined to create a reader's dream. Large overstuffed chairs were littered about the space. The Christmas lights under the balcony walkways created a fairylike appeal to readers who snuggled up with cups of artesian coffees. Book club members were chatting, children were reading, and the atmosphere was inviting.

"I have never seen anything like this," the stranger said.

"Come on in and have a look," Janie told him. "Welcome

to The Roxy: Books, Comics and More. It is the perfect bookstore where we encourage readers to pick up a book and turn the page."

-Fin-

Bonus Reads

Discover my other multi-cultural reads with
The Cost to Play and *Friends with Benefits*.

Olivia Gaines

Bonus Chapters: The Cost to Play

THE COST to Play

Two Cosplayers set out to create the perfect comic book, but find that they are also perfect for each other.

Olivia Gaines

Chapter 1 -

There are some daybreaks when a body awakens and is ready for the day to commence. It was going to be one of those mornings when a girl felt like she had just stepped into a scene in a Disney movie. The day would begin with that perfect quaint scene in the movie where blue birds fluttered about, flowers bloomed as the pretty girl walked by, and a tune filled the lungs exhibiting how great a girl was feeling. Jayne Wright's mood was just that good as she parked her Chevy Equinox on the street. Today, nothing could dampen her spirit. She began to sing as she made her way to the office. She bobbed her head to the left, swayed her hips to the right, and moved her shoulders to an imaginary beat as she belted out a few notes to an old R & B song. This day could not be more perfect.

"Yo baby! You lucky you got an ass like that. It almost makes up for your singing and dancing," said some man rolling by in a wheelchair on the sidewalk. Jayne gulped as if she had just swallowed a very large bug. The old fart didn't even bother to look back as he continued to roll down the sidewalk, now singing the same song, but in tune and in key. Even Wheelchair Willie's snarky comment was not going to ruin her day.

Friends often mocked her for giving every person a funny moniker, but it was her thing. It did not matter to Jayne in the least about whether she met with other's expectations of her. It was irrelevant. She was her own person, with her own mind, and her own way of doing things. Her Grandma Pearl often chided her mother, "that's what you get for naming a black Chile Jayne." She liked her name and the person she had grown up to be. Independent, free thinking, and a very talented artist.

Unfortunately her talent on paper did not translate to her abilities with humans. It was even worse when it came to humans of the opposite sex. Her inability to understand and

The Cost to Play

relate to men who wanted her as an arm piece befuddled her mind. It was almost a rude shock to her existence when a man would take her to dinner and make bumbling attempts to have her for dessert. Jayne LaQueeda Wright was not that type of woman. Most days, she wasn't sure what type of woman she was exactly, but it wasn't one that was easy.

Simplicity, however, was how she lived her life. Cawley Public Relations had been her first real job out of college and five years later she was still there. Serving as the lead designer and project manager, her work was on billboards all over Augusta, Georgia. Grandma Pearl even swore she saw an ad in Atlanta as well. It was humorous to her, even though she tried several times to explain it to her Grammy, only a handful of their clients were local. When she returned home one evening with her Clio award, Grandma Pearl whipped out *the bottle* of champagne. Jayne had a hell of a time stopping her Grammy from opening it, considering she had purchased the $3 bottle of Champale when Jayne was still in elementary school. There was no way on God's green earth that she would even partake of that sour bottle of pink vinegar. Instead, Jayne had shown up with an unopened bottle of Dom Perignon. Knowing the frugality of her Grammy, she also brought along a $13 bottle of Freixenet as her back up. Much as she had suspected, Grammy opted for the Freixenet. The bottle of Dom was still in the back of her fridge.

Soon, she promised herself, there would be something to celebrate and someone special to celebrate with. She just had to be patient. Grammy had taught her years ago not to ask God for something and then sit around like a fool worrying about it. "Let go and let God," Grandma Pearl always said, and she learned.

In high school, when the captain of the math club wanted to go all the way and she was not ready, she heeded her Grammy's words and let Ralph go. The adage still buzzed in her head in college, when the chair of the art department said he would give her a "D" in the class if she would not stay for some extracurricular activities. His activities included helping him relieve the tension in his pants. Jayne took it to God in prayer and left it there. After her professor awarded her the "D" for the course, Jayne took her cell phone and classwork to the Dean and played back the professor's request. At the end of the conference between the three of them, the Dean and her professor, both agreed she deserved that "A".

She loved her Grammy and her wisdom, but Jayne firmly believed that the good Lord helps those who help themselves. Currently, her vision in self-help included a comic book with a kick ass female superhero and matching costume that would be available in local retail stores. Outside of Bling and Storm, there were very few black female heroines in comic books and she wanted to change that. Change would come after she figured out how to make it all happen. She had the talent, but the confidence to do it was another hairy animal.

In the office, she arrived right on time to her desk, with coffee in hand and still a song in her heart. Today, she was leaving for Columbia, South Carolina to attend an anime conference called Banzaicon. This would be her first conference, or con for short, where she would dress in costume for role play. Jayne had two costumes in her car; one for tonight's ball and one for judging. The one for judging she had made herself and was rather proud of it. Nothing could ruin her morning.

Or at least, so she thought. The second hairy animal she had to contend with weekly, was her pod mate and fellow project leader, Frankie Vale, who was a very flatulent man. It did not matter what he ate, or how much or how little he put away. The man was a walking gas giant of methane. It was not just any gas, but the kind of farts that made your eyes water. One day it was so horrendous, she could have sworn his last rip of odiferous death had removed her eyebrows. It made their work relationship contentious. At one point, Jayne had created an online comic strip of Franc the Farter, who was a crime fighter that used noxious fumes to eradicate his enemy. The strip had become very popular, but Jayne forgot to use a pseudonym.

Frankie threatened to sue her if she did not take it down. She threatened to sue him for attempted murder with his fumes. He stopped talking to her, relegating their communications to necessity only.

It did not matter much anymore. She brought a face mask for when they had to work together and often after lunch. She opted to work in the conference room when it was not in use. It was easier for them both and definitely easier on her nose.

She kept her eye on the clock as she closed out her daily work At 11:58. She yelled into the bullpen, "Have a great weekend!" Jayne had sent in her monies for the cost of admission into the con. It was time to play dress up and Jayne was ready to make her mark.

- Chapter 2 -

"Professor!" she exclaimed. She stuck her arm high in the air, as if her fingers could touch the ceiling. When she received no response, she called him again stretching her arm even higher, "Professor! Professor!" She was reacting as a small child in need of a bathroom break, wiggling in the seat. Slowly he looked up. First at the clock, then at Mary Elizabeth, whom he privately named *The Riddler*. As he made his way toward her work station, thoughts of freedom floated through his mind. Only three hours left in the work day.

"Yes, Ms. Jones? How goes your project?" He looked over her shoulder at the computer monitor, visually perplexed at what he was seeing. Today's assignment was to draw the *Popliteal Fossa* to include the nerves, but what he saw on screen closely resembled a diagram on how to steal cable. Stern, firm, and with some tempered resolution, he finally responded, "No, Ms. Jones. You are somewhat off in your drawing. Please consult my instructions and begin again." Mary Elizabeth opened her mouth to protest, but the look he gave her provided caution and did not elicit the reaction she wanted. She too was aware that the professor wanted no part of her shenanigans.

Dr. Toshi Yamaguchi was one, if not the third best, medical illustrator in the country. In his fifth year as Associate Professor at Georgia Regents University in Augusta, he remained firm and detached, but highly proficient in teaching, writing, and publishing. He was on the fast track to tenure. As a Yale graduate, he had many choices of what he wanted to do and where he wanted to teach. At the age of 30, his real dream was comics. In an ideal world, he would be on staff at Marvel as the lead artist for his own original designs and characters.

In this world, he had broken his wrist in a motorcycle accident, causing some damage to the nerves in his right hand. His parents were broken hearted that he would never be able to hold a scalpel, which was fine by him, but it also limited his ability to hold charcoals, paint brushes, and colored pencils. It wasn't really such a disappointment to Toshi, since he had not truly wanted to be a doctor. In all honesty, he didn't desire to be an academic either. Even though he had the letters, people called him doctor, and his parents were appeased. Somewhat. They now craved grandchildren.

It wasn't about to happen. He liked being single. He loved the freedom to move about and spend his money as he saw fit. The small student loans he had taken out for his education were paid off. The down payment for his house was still in a bank account drawing interest and there was no one to nag him about where he was going this weekend, or why he was spending so much money on frivolous items so he could play dress up.

To Toshi Yamaguchi, fandom was about more than dressing up as your favorite hero. Fandom was a way of life, but also an expensive hobby. His girlfriend Ai, often complains when he departs for conferences for several days, stating that he is going to go broke frolicking with his friends. Often he would joke with her about fandom, coming back with a quick retort, "it costs to play with the big boys."

Ai reminds him weekly that it costs to play with a grown

woman as well. In his mind, Ai was an unwanted expense and a distraction. The sex was mediocre, leaving her place in his space, dwindling in value. Toshi checked the clock again. It was almost time. "Do not forget your homework assignments which are due on Tuesday. Remember the upper and lower lateral and medial borders of the *Popliteal Fossa* are due in eAssignment and hard copy in color when you walk in the door."

Mary Elizabeth's hand flew up again, but Toshi ignored her. Many of his student surveys would come back, with comments that he appeared to be unfeeling. That was untrue. He felt everything. Right now, the main emotion coursing through his body was disdain. Mary Elizabeth had a crush on him and used any means she could find to get his attention. He'd had it and he wanted her out the door. It was time for the weekend and he had a conference to get to as well as a Samurai suit to get packed. "Have a great weekend," he told the students as they walked out the door. He looked at Mary Elizabeth, "If you are thinking about how to complete the assignment, then you are thinking too much. Draw, draw, and draw some more." A quick closing of his MacBook and he was out the door. He popped his head into his office and waved goodbye to the office assistant, Ms. Banks, before heading to the parking garage.

Before he reached the car, he received a call from Ai. "Toshi, we need to talk." Again, another distraction. He responded in a quick clipped tone, "Fine. Meet me at 5 at the Soy Noodle House on Broad Street." He did not give her a chance to respond. He hung up and hurried home. Everything was ready to go, he just needed to load the car. He was on his way to Columbia, South Carolina for

Banzaicon. This was the first con where he was entering the costume competition. The larger cons are intimidating to some people and even more so to Toshi as an academic, but at this con he was ready to take on the challenge. He had never been to a smaller conference and was excited to debut his new Silver Samurai costume.

In his heart, at each conference he attended, he hoped to find a friend, or someone who understood him. Someone who would appreciate the craftsmanship of his homemade suit. He knew that Ai, was never going to be that person.

Toshi arrived at the Soy Noodle House at 4:50 and picked a table in the corner close to the window, but also close to the front door. In his mind, this conversation was going to be short. Ai arrived five minutes later, still wearing her work clothing and lab coat. At five foot seven with shiny black hair, a perfect set of teeth and a warm smile, Toshi was filled with regret that he could not find it in himself to love her the way she deserved to be loved. Ai Tomita was a great dentist who was loved by all of her patients, anyone who came into contact with her, and others who thrived just being in her light. Yet for Toshi, he felt dim whenever he was with her; further playing into the irony of their relationship. It was more troubling to him that her name meant "love". For him, he could only get as far as a cordial fondness for her. She whined incessantly about him being cold and unfeeling, but he did not know how to express to her that he had strong feelings about almost everything else. As she walked up to the door, his heart should have skipped a beat to see her approaching, instead what he felt bordered on apathy.

He rose to greet Ai, helping her with her chair, before reseating himself. He had already ordered a pot of hot tea. She poured him a fresh cup and one for herself. There it was, that condescending sigh. It was a sound that curled his toes inside his shoes. A sound of disappointment and angst in one exhalation, followed by a cluck of her tongue and a nibble on her bottom lip. Then came the condescending words that grabbed a man by his balls and shook him to his core. The private nickname he had given her was *Ball Buster*. "Toshi, I was hoping that this weekend you would change your mind about the *play thing* in Columbia and go with me to Atlanta, to be with our friends."

Ai's condescending attitude had rubbed him the wrong way, especially the way she said *play thing*. He wondered how much it would hurt her feelings if she knew he felt pretty much the same about her role in his life. At this point in this relationship, Toshi had already resigned himself to be free, which made him fail to filter his words. "I was hoping you would change your mind and come with me."

Ai sipped at her tea, "I am sorry, but I must say this. You are going to have to decide Toshi. Either we will have a life together, or you can continue to play your dress up superhero games."

"Fine," he said, as he returned his teacup to its saucer and rose to leave.

She was shocked. "So does this mean you are coming to Atlanta with me?" He rested his hand upon her shoulder, giving her a saddened look.

"No, it means that I am headed to Columbia to do my *play thing*."

The Cost to Play

Ai's mouth was moving but no words were coming out. Toshi leaned forward, taking her chin in his hand, while pushing the flailing jaws together. "Let me help you Ai. It means that I am not choosing you."

She stared at him with lips now taut. He made an attempt to soften the blow. "I like you enough to let you go so that you can be with someone else, who can be all the things you want and need in a husband." He lowered his head and placed a light kiss upon her cheek. He was going to be late to the ball if he didn't get a move on.

Before Ai could say anything to him, he stood in front of the window and took out his cell phone. She watched his practiced fingers move across the screen, and knew he had turned it off for the weekend. It was one of the many traits that bugged her to no end about Toshi, but indecisiveness was not one of them. Once he made up his mind that was the end.

Toshi Yamaguchi had just dumped her. When he had to make the choice between dressing up as a crime fighting superhero and drawing comics, or being with her, he opted to be the superhero. In her mind, his actions were villainous. He had just made a down payment on a new enemy and she was not going to let this go lightly. There would be no way to explain to her parents how she had managed to run off another potential husband.

Chapter 3

At 4:00 pm on Friday afternoon, Toshi dressed as Gambit from the X-Men and headed downstairs to the hotel lobby to mix and mingle with the other conference attendees. Many con junkies came early to meet the prettiest ladies and maybe score a conference hook up. This had only happened twice for him, but he was single again, so his mind was open to the possibilities. Slipping into the black seamless pants, and picking up a deck of cards, he would hold up an ace of spades to any woman who caught his eye. Thus far, there had been only two. So many of these attendees were very young and if any reminded him of a student, he shied away.

Vendors had set up earlier in the afternoon. At such a small con, there aren't many writers, artists, or designers present, but Toshi had been tapped to teach two of the classes on Saturday. One in the morning and the other in the afternoon. He was looking forward to it. As he passed by the vendor room, he nearly kept walking but was halted by a vision of delightfulness bent over into a bin of buttons and tchotchkes. In his mind, he hoped it was a woman. The purple Lycra pants, black hair, and a glimpse of side boob said female. It would be most uncomfortable for him if she were not. Feeling confident, he leaned down and whispered close to her ear, "that has to be the most perfect ass I have ever seen."

The princess with the perfect posterior turned slowly, raised her body to full height, and faced Toshi with a look of disgust, "you do realize you said that out loud, right?"

The directness of her tone made Toshi step back. He

The Cost to Play

was also surprised to see that she was a black woman, with a whole lot of attitude. The heels she wore gave her an additional few inches in height, but he imagined her in stocking feet to stand only at five feet maybe four inches. She had full lips and deep, wide set brown eyes that looked like pools of liquid milk chocolate. She had a gap in her teeth and the cutest nose he had ever seen on any woman. Initially, he had thought the hair to be a wig, but as he stared at her, it did not take long to understand it was actually her hair.

"I meant to say it loud enough for you to hear me," he added with a cockiness that was unlike him. Being dressed as Gambit, he felt stronger, more powerful, and far more daring than he should. "At least I didn't ask you to sit it in my lap." He stood with his legs shoulder width apart, his arms folded across his midriff, calling her out. By making such a bold move, Toshi also noticed that his heart rate had increased.

Toshi thought she looked extremely hot dressed as Bling, and much like the comic book character, attitude and angst radiated from her. Jayne was staring at the costumed man, but it was unclear if behind the mask he was Japanese or Chinese. What was evident was the man was arrogant and thought she was an easy mark. She moved closer to him, bringing a smaller smile to his face as she extended her index finger, wiggling it, beckoning him to come closer. "I like the costume Gambit and I like how you decided to take a gamble, but I have to let you know something very important." She paused to drive home the words she was going to hit him with, "but...."

Toshi leaned closer to hear what she had to say. He placed his hand upon his chest in mock chivalry, but it was really an effort to quell the rapid beating of his heart. She smiled as she delivered the words, "you are an asshole."

He reacted as if he had been slapped. She pushed him to the side and walked passed him heading into the conference registration area. He watched her sashay away with more than a casual interest. The initial assessment had not changed. That was still the most perfect ass he had ever seen in his life, but the woman who owned it, was a handful. He found himself with a very wide grin that harbored a very playful thought. *That ass was a perfect handful as well.*

Toshi felt stimulated by her. Her words had hurt his feelings. That was something that had never happened before and he did not like the idea of her thinking of him as an asshole. He called after her. "There you go again, just walking away from the team."

The lady stopped dead in her tracks. Giving just enough of a turn. "I was never truly a part of the team."

She walked away. The faint scent of her perfume still lingered in the air. It was mixed with whatever she used on her hair. Toshi's body reacted. Emotions flooded through him and confusion was knocking at the chunks of blockades that had grown into his cerebral cortex. He had slept with a black woman before, actually, all races of women, but never really considered it anything other than a physical release. Yet that creamy skinned vixen, moved him. For the first time in several years, he felt something stirring him up.

This was going to be a great weekend.

Jayne was an artist and a very good one, but there were

The Cost to Play

two things Jayne was not; easy and easy going. Comic books and painting were her first love, cosplaying was her second, with costume designing coming in a close third. Men were something she had little time for, although her body frequently reminded her of the important role they played in the life of a woman. More so if she planned to procreate. However, children were nowhere on her list of things to get done in her lifetime. Her experience with men had been limited, with only one serious sexual partner to her credit, whom she seldom spoke of nor had many fond memories. Alex had been the first man she been intimate with. Time was moving along at such a clip, that there was little time left to worry about the insignificance of a warm body next to her in bed. Although most conferences served as hookups for the lonely and disenfranchised, for her, this conference was her opportunity to display her newest anime outfit, make a few contacts, and hopefully have a remote chance of winning a prize.

The insulting man in the vendor shop had been just another testosterone filled moron who wanted to get into her pants before getting into her head. Her eyes grew wide at the mere thought of the stories she could tell about the misunderstandings from men who wanted to be a part of her world, but really did not understand what she was trying to accomplish. Jayne wanted to be a costume designer and design an original comic book character.

She lived art. She drank art. In her free time, she breathed comics and she knew this year was going to be her swan song. This year she was going to debut her comic book even if she had to self-publish it on Kindle or Blurb. The work was good. The script was even better. The art work was high caliber, but it was lacking something. She could not put her finger on it, but there was still some time to figure out the defunct.

At 28 years old, Jayne had scored her job with Cawley Public Relations after an internship her senior year in art school. She had not planned to stay with the company for five years, but it was a good fit. Moving back home had not been an easy decision, but her Grammy was getting up in age and the break up with Alex had nearly cost her the small amount of sanity that was left over after sketching and scribbling fictional characters. Occasionally, she would make it to a con and get to dress up as one of her favorite characters as well.

Cosplaying to her was a step beyond *LARPing* and far more fun. Cosplay was a great way for costume designers to get together and show off their craft. The conferences allowed other comic book, fantasy, and science fiction lovers to get together and play games. To her, there was a big difference between cosplaying and LARPing. LARPing is live action role-playing, where the characters actually create scenarios and reenact scenes. That was just a bit too geeky for Jayne's taste. However, getting a chance to don a costume and become the character, changed the way she felt about herself. She loved how the costumes made her feel. In costume, she was powerful and pretty.

Commanding. Admired. Loved.

None of the things she exhibited in real life. In real life, she was a petite weird black woman, with crazy hair, a gap in her teeth and dreams that men did not understand. Even her mother didn't understand her. She felt at times that her friends were humoring her when they listened to her stories. Eventually, she had stopped sharing her ideas. None of what she said was coming to fruition, so it was all just a pipe dream. Or so it had been. This weekend, she was going to change her fate. Winning this costume contest was going to change her storyline. This was going to move her dream forward.

Something made her come to a stop. Besides the several people wanting to take photos with her, she felt eyes boring into her back. Slowly she turned around and spotted the Gambit dude still watching her. Camera flashes were going off as she posed with a few children, two men, and the last one she took, she posed in a fighting stance. The shock she felt when she realized she was posing with Gambit was almost too much. The charge between the two of them was palpable.

A small crowd began to gather as Gambit slid into another pose. Not to be outdone, she altered her stance to a second pose matching him. The crowd began to chant as Gambit pulled playing cards from his pockets and sent them flying into the crowd. In a flash, he grabbed her by the hand and pulled her close, segueing into a third pose that caused the crowd to go mad. He held her close with his hands in the small of her back. She could feel the power of his thighs pressing against her own while the male part of him pressed to her delicate part as he hoisted her thigh to ensure she felt his enthusiasm. The kids were all smiling. The flashes from the cameras had nearly blinded her, but she got a grip on herself. Without making a scene, Jayne pulled away, bowed to the audience, and kowtowed to Gambit, making eye contact with him while mouthing the words, "asshole."

She rounded the corner with Toshi on her heels, but the throng of people closed in on him wanting more pictures. He would not be able to get to her in time and he felt antsy, charged up, excited and ready for.......whatever. He wasn't sure. Toshi knew that whatever it was, it included that woman.

    Jayne rounded the corner, out of breath and full of conflicted emotions. When Gambit took her hand, the sparks that flew up her arm were electric. The man was a pig to even pull her in close like that, so she could feel the pure maleness of his body. It was offensive! Yet, she had never experienced such an intense feeling with anyone.

Chapter 4

    The light from the ceiling was cascading down on the dais, illuminating the strong facial features of the instructor. Jayne watched with some amusement as she eyed his strong jawline, high cheek bones, and Asian eyes. His irises were dark, giving him an aura of mystery, intrigue, and a hint of something she could not mash her finger into. Something felt familiar about him, but his skill set with shadowing was amazing. Each stroke of his wrist sparked her imagination as he tinted the panels of each comic book cell, demonstrating how to darken areas of the body to simulate motion. It was uncertain if the attraction she was feeling derived from his talent or the confidence which radiated from his role as an instructor. Either way, Dr. Toshi Yamaguchi was sexy as hell to her.

    She had never dated an Asian man, nor had any interest in doing so until now, but this man was giving her second thoughts. First that Gambit dude, now him. She thought back to her philosophy professor, who found Freudian meaning in every occurrence. She had met two very different Asian men in two days. One she found completely repulsive. The other, she found fascinating. The soft, confident way in which he delivered the two hour block of instruction was followed along with a trancelike state of conference goers. Jayne found herself hypnotized by his words and enlightened with his instruction.

    Banzaicon was only the fourth conference that Jayne had attended in her life. Outside of her run-in with that Gambit guy, she was enjoying herself immensely. After the check in on Friday night, she noticed two new classes had been added to the schedule. *Shadowing Techniques for Comics*, and *Creating Original Characters*. She jumped at the chance to take the courses. Thus far she had not been disappointed. The instructor was absolutely phenomenal as he used his tablet to sketch out designs, while having the audience follow along. Jayne was even more impressed that he left the make shift stage to walk through the room to check the progress of each of the attendee's work before he moved on to the next technique. At some instance during the instruction, it was twice as impressive that Dr. Yamaguchi laid eyes on every single drawing in the room, providing quasi one on one with every attendee in the session. This was doubly impressive, considering it was standing room only. The younger fans were eating it up, when he looked at their pages, giving canned responses of "good, a little darker here," or "great job." Jayne even found she puffed up a bit when he glanced at her work, stating "good eye for detail." Now she felt foolish because he smelled good too. She was fighting back the urge to get all goofy like many of the women on the front row were.

In the final steps of the drawing, Dr. Yamaguchi employed an old technique of using time lapse to dictate shadow. "Start your shadowing technique at noon. To simulate running, shift the shadow to two o'clock, then three in the next frame." Jayne had never considered such a thing, but when he demonstrated his idea in three panels, the whole room said, "ahhh." Before long, the two hours were up. Dr. Yamaguchi thanked everyone for coming.

The young women flocked to the instructor as Jayne sat, still sketching out an idea that had come to mind based on his last words. No other course had been planned in this room until after lunch, so she continued to work, drafting

The Cost to Play

through her ideas. She was listening, but not listening. As the instructor escorted the women to the door, his deep voice reminded her of the bad guy in the Karate movies who always came into the whore house and drank up all the Sake. He told the young ladies, "I must leave now to grab a bite to eat, before the next session. Excuse me." She found herself smiling as she mimicked, "ah, yes, Mr. Woo, so glad to have you in our fine establishment." She let out a pretend courtesan giggle like she had heard the Asian women do in the movies.

One of the young ladies asked him to join her, but he declined, saying he had already committed to having lunch with a friend. Jayne heard that part from his practiced lines and just imagined his new friend as some dim-witted ingénue in a Sailor Moon costume. Dr. Yamaguchi's deep voice was rich with southern undertones and dripping with the practiced ease of a very expensive education. The ladies sounded disappointed, but he turned to Jayne asking, "Are we ready my friend? I am starving."

Jayne looked over her shoulder to see who he was talking to and spying no one else in the room, she quickly realized it was her. The look on his face was asking for a rescue, which made her gather her things and say, "sure thing ole pal. Ready when you are."

He opened the outer door for her and led the way to the hotel restaurant. "I only have an hour or so before the next session, so I hope you don't mind eating here and..." he paused, cutting her a side glance. "... You do know I heard you back there?"

She gulped, lowering her head in shame at the racial stereotype she had projected, mumbling an apology. She would make it up to him over lunch. Jayne had not realized how hungry she had been until she smelled the food. The hotel restaurant did not seem like a good idea, but most of the conference attendees were headed out for pizza or sandwiches, which left the lobby seating open. Toshi pulled out a chair for her then went to the bar to grab a couple of menus.

What are you doing here with him? Wild thoughts ran through her mind that it was going to be the prickliest lunch ever, but to her surprise it was not. The conversation was light after he thanked her for coming to his rescue. His voice remained steady as he said, "I love to attend cons, but I am uncertain if many of the attendees are even old enough to drink, so I err on the side of caution."

"You seem to have a great number of groupies for an artist."

He smiled as he raised his hand for the waiter to come over. "Art is sexy. I am an artist." He arched an eyebrow indicating that she needed to deduct the final formula.

"You are a sexy artist," she said in a flat voice. It was more of a question than a logical deduction.

"Really, you think so? I thank you." He let out a chuckle before adding, "have you decided what you would like?"

Jayne looked at the menu and decided on a Chicken Caesar Salad, as she watched him over the rim of her glasses. He ordered a pot of tea. Since she had been insulting before, she felt she needed him to understand that she was not ignorant of his culture. When the tea arrived, she stood and kowtowed to him while filling his tea cup. She poured a bit for herself, then took a seat. He watched her with some interest, but his facial expressions were indecipherable.

As the food arrived, he ate rice with chopped vegetables

The Cost to Play

and Sautéed Chicken, as he reviewed notes and sketches. It felt peculiar to sit here like this with him, sharing a meal, yet it was perfectly comfortable. They were sharing a space, but not sharing each other. He had not asked her name and she had not volunteered to provide him with it.

She looked up from her salad and found him staring at her. "What?" she asked.

"There is something about you that speaks to me," he said as he cut into the last chunk of chicken.

Jayne wasn't sure if it was a pick up line or another smart ass comment. "Thank you," was all she could muster. He sat there waiting for her to say something.

"What?"

"I don't know," he said as he shrugged his shoulders. "There is something about you. Your qi is calling to me." His heart rate had picked up again. This was an uncommon reaction for him around a woman. Although he had been with a few black women before, she *felt* different. It unsettled him.

"I thought Chi was a Chinese term," she said while continuing to eat her meal but looked at her watch.

"Qi, or, chi and even Xi, are terms that are in several languages. All meaning life force. I don't know what it is about you...." His words trailed off as he eyed the check.

There was a quick demonstration on Kimono making in one of the break out rooms that she wanted to see before going to his next session on creating original characters. She picked up her purse, grabbed a twenty from her wallet, and laid it on the table. "Well, today is not the day for you to figure it out." She bowed again and told him to take care as she headed down the hall to the demonstration.

There was something about him as well that made her

feel off kilter. She didn't like it... not one bit. Playing with a man like that always came at a price and she was unwilling to pay the toll.

The afternoon class was equally phenomenal as Dr. Yamaguchi showed the attendees how to use a favorite personal photo as a template to create an original character. The sound of pencils against sketch pads making strokes and shading, radiated throughout the crowded room. As he had earlier in the morning, Toshi milled through the throng of sketchers, who had laid out on the floor, leaned against the walls, and occupied every chair, as they presented their work to him at the midway point. The latter portion of the session, he taught his makeshift students the importance of drawing muscles, muscle tone, and muscle sinew. Jayne was amazed at how much better her earlier sketch looked after applying these newly learned techniques. She found herself staring at him absently.

As if he felt her eyes upon him, Toshi turned, catching her unaware, meeting her gaze. His heartbeat sped up when their eyes connected. *What was it about this woman?* He quickly shifted his focus so his body would not betray him. At the end of the session, he was flocked by conference goers with a ton of questions. He looked for her, but she had disappeared.

Jayne was uncomfortable with the intensity of the connection she was feeling with the good doctor. Maybe she was responding to his artistic ability. It was a foolhardy assessment. The woman in her was responding

The Cost to Play

to the man in him. She shook it off and headed to her room to change for the Cosplay event at 6 pm.

Jayne was planning to debut her costume as Pirotess, from _Record of Lodoss War_. Uncertainty was ringing through her mind as she wondered if anyone would know who she was or even *get* the character. It was all she had, so she was going to go with it. Earlier, she felt a great deal of confidence. Now she was uncertain. Three weeks had been spent creating the costume, ensuring that every minute detail had been covered, even working her body out extra hard. Threads, stitches, and fabric choice were all very important when designing a costume. Even more important was the flow of material when on the body. It was these details that she hoped would give her a placing in the show. She checked her hair, her makeup, and adjusted the girls in the suit.

The time had flown by and it was time to head downstairs.

Entering the elevator, there were several Lolita's, *Dragon Ball Z* characters along with other sub characters from *Sailor Moon*. The show stopper was the *Silver Samurai* in the lobby. The detail of the costume was bordering on amazing as many walked up to him to touch the leather and fabricated pieces. As Jayne walked by him, he drew his sword, placing it in front of her to block her path. She could not see his face, but immediately knew it was the jerk from last night who was dressed as Gambit. A quick shove with her hand and she pushed the sword aside and made her way to the judging stage. The costumes had been judged earlier yesterday, so tonight was just a formality.

One by one the characters filed on stage, role-playing in

the costumes and showing off their handy work. The Silver Samurai was a skilled martial artist and swordsman. The audience oohed and ahhed as he maneuvered from posing to performing high flying kicks for two and a half minutes. Jayne felt sexy as Pirotess when she climbed on stage. She posed and showed a bit of skin as she sauntered across the platform.

The waiting was brief since many of the costumes had already been judged. Three of the *Dragon Ball Z* characters had placed with honorable mentions. An online comic series had received third place for one of the characters, which received a great audience response. Jayne was excited when she was awarded second place. The Silver Samurai received first place. Standing close to him, she understood why. He looked really good in the costume with his muscles bulging through the taut leather, his shiny black hair hanging from under the helmet, and those intense eyes gazing through the eye slots.

The winners were all lined up on stage for a quick photo op and then the group began to disperse. The samurai touched her arm beckoning her to follow him. She trailed him into a corner and he removed his helmet. Jayne's eyes were wide when she realized Gambit, the Silver Samurai, and Dr. Toshi Yamaguchi was the same person!

Toshi asked her, "What are your plans for tonight?"

"I plan to go to the party and have a drink or two," she told him waiting to see if he would ask her to dinner.

"I am heading to my room." He turned and began to walk away. "Come with me." It was said with such matter-of-factness that Jayne stood there blinking after him. He looked back to see why she was not walking along with him. He extended to her his hand in a quieter request.

"What am I going to do in your room?"

Toshi's eyebrows went up, "I was hoping... me."

She couldn't believe it. "You know you said that out loud?"

Toshi moved closer to her. "Would it have more impact if I whispered it instead?"

Jayne was disgusted with him. All of her admiration for his talent had flown out the window. She tried to step around him, but he extended his hand to stop her. "There is something about you that stirs my blood. I want to be with you. I am being honest by telling you what I want."

"It seems like you would want to know my name first, Professor. And you know what...?" she paused with her hand on her hip. "I was wrong about you. You are not an asshole, you are a *fucking* asshole."

Toshi moved so quickly Jayne was startled. He stood toe to toe with her. His breath, caressing her cheek as he leaned into her ear. "Pirotess, Bling, or whatever you want to be called, you are amazing. You are a talented artist and you are making me crazy, but I understand. There have been so many men that have lied to you. The truth is hard for you to accept."

"I can accept the truth just fine. I don't accept you wanting to use me as a personal plaything."

He lowered his voice to a whisper, using a sensual and sultry tone. "I don't plan to use you. I plan to give you hours of pleasure." He said it in such a way, that her body said yes, but her mouth said, "thanks, but no."

She stepped around him and headed for the elevator. The idea of going to the party no longer seemed fun. In the morning she would check out and head home. That jerk off had just ruined her night. She hoped he spent the rest of the night doing just that as well.

Unfortunately, her wish for him would probably not come true. A flock of women surrounded him. Some were subtle, while others were direct, using their bodies to gain his attention. She looked back at him once more and was surprised to see his attention was not on the women, but instead on her. Jayne's brain was screaming at her to keep moving, but her body was crying, begging her to go back. She shook her head at him, then moved on to the elevator.

Bonus Chapters: Friends with Benefits

Friends with Benefits

Olivia Gaines

Chapter One

The view from the balcony was often an inviting scene. Below, lounging about the pool, were beautiful people who wanted to be seen or were waiting patiently to be picked up and made relevant. The climb to importance in standing and social status which would be determined by the longevity of the next person they chose as a bed partner. If chosen correctly, a book deal or a reality show could be possible, but it took time. It took money. It took the right clothing, but more importantly, it took being seen with the right person.

For him, the beautiful people were as misleading as the pool itself; crystalline and inviting, but filled with bacteria. Caution was not germane to the chemicals and salts that the staff added to keep down the algae and fungi, because at the end of the day, someone always pees in the pool. In the middle of the night moans and grunts could be heard by people who think it is a good idea to copulate in water. He never swam in the pool, nor ventured to lounge at its side. The whole area was shark-infested and at times, he felt like a defenseless guppy.

Modern relationships had become confusing and left him wanting. What he yearned for and wanted was unclear, but it was very clear that he no longer wanted what he was receiving. As he stood on the balcony, he noticed the ample-chested young beauty eyeing him. He raised his beer bottle to acknowledge that she had been seen. She raised her bikini top to extend an invitation for him to come downstairs to see more. A nod of his head was given to the young ingénue, before he retreated into his

Friends with Benefits

condo, closed the blinds and turned on the game. That was some nonsense he wanted no part of; been there, did her.

It had crossed his mind on several occasions to put the condo up for sale and purchase a three- or four-bedroom home in Marietta or Kennesaw to get out of the city. He definitely needed to get out of this building, since he had slept with almost every single female tenant. Married women often invited him for coffee, pie or some other obscure reason to enter their front door, so in the middle of the night or the afternoon, he could slip out the back. As much as it pained him to say, he was tired of sex.

Copulation had begun to feel like a chore more than a want or a need. Today was one of those days when he neither needed nor wanted any. A private challenge was issued to himself; it was time to find out how long he could actually go without sex. The laptop sat on the table and a quick flip of the top, opened an application and printed out this and next month's calendar. It had already been a week, so he crossed those days off on the calendar and took them to the kitchen to pin them on the fridge. This could be done; he needed to know what he was made of and how much sex actually influenced his decision-making ability.

Grayson Broche took pride in his appearance although his hair was never quite combed. He always felt that his slightly disheveled locks added to his tall, swarthy appeal, adding an air of mystery to him. Few people could even fathom that he was an entertainment lawyer who represented some of the biggest acts in the movie and the music industry. Others could not understand how he lived in Atlanta and represented those who worked in

Hollywood. It was simple, word of mouth. He was good. His team was better. He was an attorney who was honest.

The days of hands-on with the talent were behind him and he only dealt with producers, management and the upper echelons of the business. Young actors and talent still trying to find themselves were old hat and old news. The phone calls in the middle of the night from starlets who were drinking and driving, incarcerated or plain inebriated, no longer had his number. It seemed so difficult for them to understand, as an entertainment lawyer, he negotiated their contracts and took a percentage. He was not their parent and he was not interested in babysitting their neurosis. Eleven years in the business of entertainment law had taught him one cardinal rule: never sleep with the help.

As a young man, fresh out of law school, many thought he was nuts to open his own firm without any seasoning. Who needed seasoning when you already knew the flavoring? Many young artists were being ripped off and cheated by unscrupulous business practices and companies who took advantage of their naiveté. Broche & Associates specialized in artists across all genres including stage, television, music, film, and even production. Grayson's reputation was sound, his practices, fair and his team was completely above par. It was instilled in every person who worked with and for him: hands off the talent. Friends, groupies and tagalongs were okay, but the clientele was a no-no. Sex complicated matters. When matters become complicated, so does the money. He made it abundantly clear to the team—don't screw with my money.

Overall, Grayson considered himself to be a good guy with a few bad habits. His main fault was he had poor taste in women. At 36 years old, he was ready for something different, but he had to have some clarity on where he was going. His best friend Charlize often told him he thinks with his eyes. Grayson had no idea what that meant, but she was the only constant in his life. They had a ten-year friendship built on trust, understanding, and no hanky-panky. Charlize was Grayson's rock and his best friend.

And that is what prompted Grayson Broche to start thinking a bit differently.

Chapter Two

Charlize climbed onto the flexion distraction table to begin the realignment of the quarterback's right hip. She was amazed at how whiny he was during treatment and how tough he seemed on the field in last week's Falcon's game. After positioning herself under his thigh, she hooked her arm under his shoulder and counted to three. One push, a shove and a twist, she heard the familiar pop while watching relief wash over Mr. Crybaby's face.

For the past five years she had served as one of the sports medicine doctors for the Atlanta Falcons. Doc Feelme was the nickname the players gave her, but Dr. Charlize Filleman is the best in the field. It was a bidding war for her talent between the Braves, the Hawks, the Thrashers and the Falcons to get her on staff. What made her a hot commodity was she was a certified chiropractor as well as a licensed M.D. She worked on the best bodies in the business and was surrounded by rich men with too much money and gigantic egos. Women were always flocking around the training camps trying to be seen, or wanting to be a trophy. It all disgusted her.

On occasions, during the off season, Charlize prided herself on getting away for a fabulous vacation, then back to work. The thought had crossed her mind to open her own practice and patent some of her training techniques, but last year, her best friend Grayson had convinced her to write a cookbook for the pro athlete. With his connections, he scored her a sweet book deal and personally represented her in the negotiations. He was a great friend and the type of guy who had principles. He taught her early on when she took the job with the team, don't sleep with the help—

it diminishes your authority.

It was great advice. The players often asked her out or bought her expensive gifts that she refused. She watched several of the physical therapists on her staff get entangled with the athletes only to be humiliated in the end when the player married some real housewife of Atlanta type. New staff members were warned in orientation, "I am the standard, do as I do, and you will have a long career. Please, be smart, don't sleep with the players. If you fraternize, you are fired. I will not bother to hear your side of the story, you are gone."

Why she bothered was beyond her; every season, there was always one. It took her two seasons to get smart and only hired women who were not into men, or women who were a couple of steps below attractive. It was unfair, but it cut down on fraternization and stabilized her staff. The past three years, the team came back to camp with the same therapist which made all involved happy; without a learning curve, worked moved at the right pace.

Charlize just wished she was happy as well and could find someone who could also move at her speed. She had not dated in three years and was completely bored with the dating process. It befuddled her to no end why men believed that dinner and a movie equated to coming to her home and bouncing up and down on her all night. It was not her style. A connection had to be present. There had to be respect, understanding, and a spark. Heck, she would be happy to have dinner and conversation about something other than football. She worked with the team. She didn't play *on* the team. *No*, I cannot get you an autograph. *No*, I will not tell you a player's physical condition so you can bet on the game. And I will definitely, never, sneak you a picture of a player during the rehabilitation process.

The only male company she kept in the past three years was her weekly dinners with Grayson. The conversations were lively, the access he had to shows were phenomenal and she truly felt his friendship was one of the more precious things in her life. She never wanted it to be complicated or convoluted. She was honest with him when she did not understand some of his choices in women, but never questioned, just supported, and was there to pick up the pieces when it inevitably went awry. This year, she was planning a nice getaway to Kauai, and had considered asking him to come along; she just wasn't sure how he would take it. Also under consideration, during the holidays, his family always had big lavish spreads, and she was uncertain if he wanted to forgo the annual tradition for some exotic sun. She smiled when she thought of him; a bright spot in her life.

He must have been thinking about her as well, her cell phone chimed and she answered on the second ring, "Howdy, Partner!"

"You free for dinner tonight?"

"Sure, my place or yours?"

"You come to me, and bring some wine, all I have is beer."

Charlize knew the tone in his voice, something was on his mind. She shut everything down in the office and headed home first for a change of clothing. When he asked for the bottle of wine, she knew they would empty it and she would be staying over in the guest room. Whatever was on his mind must be a dilemma that was heavily weighted, she just hoped it wasn't another love interest gone wrong.

Chapter Three

Grayson's condo was located in midtown Atlanta in the heart of the mass of traffic, college students, and aspiring artists. His office was not far away from his home and Grayson often rode his motorcycle into work. Most of his clientele thought he was attempting to portray the proverbial bad boy with the Valkyrie, and was almost disappointed when they found out that he rode it mainly to save on gas. Charlize often laughed because her friend was such a dude.

During her first visit to his condo, she was not surprised to find the black leather couch, glass end tables, and statues of a large bathing Hebe. The painting over the couch was homage to the 80's and the bedroom was reminiscent of a broke pimp's younger days. It was the leather padded headboard decorated with purple studs which made her laugh out loud. The only thing worse were the bedside lamps which were covered in red velvet and the shades were embossed with the words L.O.V.E. and cut out hearts. When the lamps were turned on, they cast L.O.V.E. on the walls. Without even thinking, she unplugged both lamps and took them to the trash; he attempted to argue and she held up her finger for him to be quiet. There could be no logic, reasoning, or rationale for such hideous items. Purse and keys in hand she only said, "car, now...." and drove him to a furniture store. Together, they chose a soft brown suede sofa and matching recliner with a cherry wood coffee table accented with strong, clean lines. As her gift to him, she purchased the matching ottoman and end tables, and bought two new lamps for his bedroom. A gentle nudge was provided and Grayson was convinced that the new headboard was his idea.

While they were out, Charlize pointed out the matching bookcases which would be perfect for his media collection and books. The paintings were replaced by show posters autographed by his clients. The bathing Hebe was replaced by a ficus and some dieffenbachia's, which flourished in the morning sun. The leather couches were moved to the third bedroom which now served as a man cave. The hideous headboard was now in the guest bedroom along with the sexist end tables that said "seduce me." To her surprise, Grayson asked for her assistance in picking out an appropriately sized dining room set to compliment the new living room furniture. It made her heart happy to rid his home of the glass and wrought iron set with the matching fabric covered chairs. His home now looked like a settled and established gentleman lived in it, versus a love shack for the misunderstood.

The kitchen was her favorite. For a condo, it was far roomier and more spacious than expected. Grayson had made great choices on the appliances; they considered themselves foodies who loved to cook and very rarely ate out. One thing the two friends truly shared in common was a love of health and nutrition. Each week, they sought a new recipe to try out and the best selections were chosen and put to the side. After many years, the box of recipes which had been tweaked and adjusted were now sorted and being added to her new cookbook.

Tonight, for dinner they were making roast pork with sage and pecan pesto, green beans with toasted almonds with lemon and dessert was a fruit salad with lemon mint syrup. It became important to Charlize that nothing be wasted, each ingredient should be used completely and the meal should offer more than one serving. Grayson had already prepared the pork loin in the apple cider brine and when she arrived, they chatted while he browned the pork loin in the pan, she trimmed the green beans, minced the garlic and sautéed it in a pan.

It would take the roast an hour to cook and she opened the wine, poured them both a glass before she began to prepare the fruit for dessert. As she placed the items in the fridge, she noticed the calendar, "Are you counting down to something special?"

"Nope, those are the number of days I have not had sex," he said plainly as he wiped down the counters. Charlize dropped the glass bowl and began to check him for fever. "Wait, my medical bag is in the car, let me go and grab it," she told him as he watched her with a facial expression that was less than amused. He added the pecans, sage and other ingredients into the food processor to make the pesto, now he was feeling a little insecure for sharing this with her so soon. It had only been 14 days. This wasn't a big feat for him, but his mind was clearer. He cleaned up the glass from the floor and went over it with a Swiffer to pick up any remaining shards.

Charlize realized he was serious and apologized, "I'm sorry, I thought maybe something was wrong."

"Something is wrong," he said as he pulsed the processor, "it's my personal life; right now, the only good thing in it, is you."

"That's really sweet, but seriously, why are you abstaining?"

"I need to know more about myself. I need some clarity. I want...."

He got quiet.

She poured more wine and waited. The years of friendship had taught her to wait for him to collect his thoughts. Working with type *A* males had also taught her to be quiet and not fill in the spaces with assumptions and idle chatter. He would tell her when he had gathered the right words.

"I want something very similar to what you and I have, but with benefits." Charlize dropped the wine glass.

And that was how Grayson Broche opened the discussion to starting a relationship that included being more than just friends.

About the Author

Olivia Gaines is the author of numerous bestselling novellas and books, including *Two Nights in Vegas*, *A Few More Nights*, and has had several number one best sellers with *The Blakemore Files* including *Being Mrs. Blakemore* and *Shopping with Mrs. Blakemore*.

She lives in Augusta, GA, with her husband, son and snotty cat, Katness Evermean.

Connect with Olivia on her Facebook page at http://on.fb.me/1eorEAr or her website at http://oliviagaines.com.

Olivia Gaines

Made in the USA
Charleston, SC
18 April 2016